"When you we——— ..., I felt safe for the first time...in a long time. Thank you."

"You're welcome," Cole whispered.

Kenzie didn't answer. Until he started to rise. He wanted to stay—to make sure she stayed safe and kept breathing those slow even breaths. But he didn't belong here with her.

"Don't leave," she whispered, her eyes still closed.

Cole swallowed the lump in his throat and settled back in his chair, her hand cradled carefully in his. Why hadn't he picked up that novel sooner? If he'd just allowed himself to trust his instincts, Kenzie's ordeal would have been shorter.

He shook his head. Kenzie would live to see another day, to light up the world with her smile. He had not been too late. That would have to be enough. Her nightmare was over.

Or was it?

JENNESS WALKER

has always loved a good story. She grew up scouting around her grandparents' basement for something good to read. Today she doesn't feel complete if she doesn't have a book nearby. When she's not reading or writing, she enjoys hanging out with her husband, playing with her part-time dog and planning trips to explore small-town America.

Jenness Walker
Double Take

Steeple
Hill®

Published by Steeple Hill Books™

STEEPLE HILL BOOKS

Steeple
Hill®

Recycling programs
for this product may
not exist in your area.

ISBN-13: 978-0-373-44360-4

DOUBLE TAKE

Printed in U.S.A.

Not by works of righteousness which we have done,
but according to His mercy He saved us.
—*Titus* 3:5

To my family—Mom and Dad; my brothers, Ben and Anthony; and my husband, Jason—for your never-failing encouragement, support and love. Thanks for believing in me.

Acknowledgments

I owe a big thank-you to Detective Mark Weaver, the perfect consultant. I owe you a lifetime of Coldstone Creamery gift cards. Also, I need to thank Dave, my mechanic; the nurses who made sure my heroine didn't accidentally die of infection; and my writing buddies—Cathy, Ava and Faith.

ONE

If her car hadn't died that morning, Monique might not have, either. But the car died. Monique boarded a bus. And the fight for her life began.

Cole Leighton shifted on the bench and closed *Obsession* to study the cover. Surely the author hadn't given away the ending already. He'd never read a Warren Flint thriller, but this one caught his attention for some reason. Maybe because of the high praise or the blurb on the back. More likely because of the cover model. He glanced at her one more time: back pressed against a wall, delicate fingers splayed against the concrete block, slim figure silhouetted by a streetlight. But it was her face that held him. The wide eyes, the fear-laced expression partially hidden by dark hair blowing in a slight breeze. She drew him in.

Heels clicked against the sidewalk. A woman advanced toward the bus stop, gesturing with one hand while holding a phone to her ear.

"Mom, I'm sorry, but there's nothing I can do about it…" Exaggerated patience sounded in her tone. "Yes, I know this is your last day in town, but my car just gave up the ghost. I'll be there, but I'm running late. Okay?"

So much for some quiet reading time. Cole gazed at the road, watching for the bus as she snapped her phone closed and sat down beside him.

She broke an awkward pause with a polite "How are you?"

He was in the middle of Atlanta. Smelling diesel fumes, fighting crowds and wishing for the hot Texas air. But he nodded and said, "Fine."

Her cell phone rang again. She groaned and silenced the ring. "Ever had one of those days where everything goes wrong?" she asked.

A wry smile tugged at Cole's lips, and he nodded. He finally turned to look her full in the face, then blinked. She looked hauntingly familiar. Where…?

She gave him a small smile.

Sucking in a breath, he tilted his head and studied her. Dark hair fell in shiny waves past her shoulders. A pale face with wide, sad eyes—

Those eyes narrowed. "Something wrong?"

Heat swept his face. Cole shook his head and looked away, down at *Obsession*'s cover again. She could be the model's twin.

Weird.

"Oh, good. Here it comes."

His bench partner pointed to a bus with orange stripes and a turquoise MARTA sign as it rounded the corner. Cole gathered his things and walked to the curb as the bus arrived. But hesitated before following her up the bus steps.

She chose a seat near the front, but, face still burning, Cole strode down the aisle. About halfway back, he dropped into an empty seat beside a James Earl Jones look-alike. His chest abnormally tight, Cole reached for the novel again.

She sat near the front and crossed her legs. One of her shoelaces dangled in the aisle, swinging like a slow pendulum as other passengers walked by. She studied the pedestrians outside the window, the way sunlight played off the apartment windows, the angle of the bus driver's hat, the warm leather of a passenger's jacket. She thought she should take a picture to help her remember this day for the rest of her life, every part of it.

She didn't.

But she would remember anyway.

The bus lurched forward, and Monique braced her hand against the seat in front of her. The gray fabric itched, but she held on, leaning into a curve. When the tree-lined road wound out of the commercial area—

Cole looked up from the page and stared at the gray fabric on the seat in front of him. Maybe he shouldn't be reading this. Not right here, right now, on a bus with the heroine's twin sitting in the second-row aisle seat. It was kind of like watching an in-flight movie with a plane crash somewhere in its plotline.

When Cole didn't settle back into the book, his seatmate took that as a cue to talk. "Beautiful day, ain't it, son? Makes me glad to be alive."

Cole followed the man's gaze to the window as the bus rounded a corner. Rays of sunlight spread through thick tree-cover, dancing over the grass of an undeveloped area.

The hair on the back of his neck prickled.

"Reminds me of home." A soft smile transformed the old man's face. "Back when my wife was alive, we used to—"

The bus swerved off the main road and ground to a halt. Out of the corner of his eye, Cole caught a flash of light—the sun glinting off metal.

This could not be happening.

But it was.

"Put your hands on the seat in front of you," a man's voice grated out. "Everyone! Hands on the seat where I can see them."

Cole spotted a second masked gunman just as a bullet tore through the roof of the bus. Someone screamed.

"I said *now!*"

"Do it, son." His seatmate sounded calm, but his withered hands trembled as he placed them on the top of the seat.

Cole obeyed, hot anger competing with cold chills.

"This is a holdup," the second man said, walking to the rear of the bus. "We don't want to hurt anyone. We just want your valuables."

Someone whimpered as a bag's contents hit the floor. A cheap pen rolled by, stopping near Cole's feet. He stared at the label and narrowed his eyes.

Why would someone hold up a bus? And why did he feel almost as if he'd known something like this was coming?

TWO

It felt like some crazy Western movie gone awry. Kenzie Jacobs gripped the seat in front of her and wished she could disappear. Her life seemed to be a series of bad days. Just when she didn't think things could get any worse…

She winced as the first gunman—the one with the leather jacket, the one who had been sitting right in front of her—shoved his weapon into the bus driver's face again.

"Get away from the radio!"

"Yes, sir," the driver said, holding his hands high.

The gunman jerked the driver to his feet, then marched him up the aisle with a gun pressed to the back of the man's head. Kenzie didn't watch. She couldn't. She closed her eyes and prayed that she wouldn't hear more gunfire, more screams, the sound of the driver's body hitting the floor.

"Keep your hands on the seats!" the second man yelled from the rear. "Heads down. No looking around. The faster we get your valuables, the faster you can get off this bus."

No shots. The driver would live another few minutes, at least.

Kenzie wished she could pull a Hollywood stunt and save the world…or at least this bus full of people. But she was never any good at saving people. So she lowered her head and closed her eyes and tried to keep the tears from pushing past her eyelids.

She didn't have anything of value with her. No jewelry. Little cash. One credit card. Even her shoes were inexpensive.

Something bumped her foot. Her eyes cracked open and she saw a gloved hand snatch her purse from the floor. The gunman breathed heavily near her ear. She could feel the heat radiating from him as he dumped her belongings. Her pocket knife hit the floor with a clatter. Lip gloss rolled to the front and thunked down the steps. A package of tissues landed near her shoes. She was glad they hadn't been open. She might need them today, if she ever made it to lunch with her mom.

When cold metal pressed against her temple, she was pretty sure she wouldn't.

The second gunman stood just in front of Cole. He could kick the thug's knees and throw his backpack over the man's face, if someone else could just go for the gun.

But the gun would go off before anyone could get it. Someone would die. And the bad guys would have to be together, or he'd have to take out the second man when the first one's back was turned. But how could he know, when he had to keep his head down? Peeking into the aisle gave him a full-on view of the man's camouflage jacket, Wolverine work boots and nothing else.

Maybe it would be all right. If everyone just relaxed, they could take the money and go, and everyone would be okay. Maybe heroics would be the wrong thing to do—would hurt people more than help.

He winced. Yeah, he was good at doing that. His gaze fell on *Obsession*—still open on his lap—and he skimmed down to where he'd left off. Where two gunmen told the bus passengers to put their heads down, their hands up, and robbed them.

No…

Where they put a gun to Monique's head. Where the bad guys jerked her to her feet, marched her down the steps. His eyes jumped to the first line again.

If her car hadn't died that morning, Monique might not have, either.

Someone was going to die.

No. It was just a crazy book. One he didn't want to read anymore. He moved his leg, jostling the book closed.

Then *he* was the one with the business end of a pistol pointing at his head.

Cole settled his foot flat on the floor again and tried to slow his breathing, but his heart raced faster. He could feel the blood pulsing in his neck as he tried to remain motionless, to fight the urge to jerk away from the weapon, to not give the gunman the wrong idea.

"Thank you for your cooperation," the man in the front finally shouted.

The gun shifted, but remained inches away from Cole's ear. With it so close, he could grab the gun first, if he got lucky. Duck and grab, then drop the guy while the seat still protected him from the first man's gaze…and weapon.

The one he could use to fire at Cole anyway. Hitting the kid in front of him, or the man next to him. His seatmate met his eyes, blinked, mouthed, "No, son."

"Don't move! Keep your hands on the seats, your heads down."

Something rustled near the front. Cole's eyes settled on the book cover, with Monique gazing up at him. Frightened. Haunted.

"We're taking one of you with us."

The whimpers grew louder.

"If you move before five minutes, if someone calls the cops, if we don't get away clean, she's dead. But if you cooperate as well as you have so far, she'll be deposited somewhere, unharmed, for the police to find."

Monique's face merged with the girl from the bench, and Cole's heart lurched.

Kenzie stood in the aisle after being jerked to her feet. Numb, she looked toward the back of the bus. The man from the bus stop met her gaze for a split second as the guy in the camo jacket held a gun to his head. Then, nothing but a sea of hands. No faces except the two men leering at her with their eyes. No one to come to her rescue.

"Come on," said the man with the leather jacket, tugging on her arm. The other guy moved toward her and pointed his weapon at a nearby child. The message was clear: Struggle, and she'd take more down with her.

She walked with leaden feet, slowly descending the stairs. Her shoe touched the tube of lip gloss, and she watched dully as it fell to the ground beside the front tire. It was her favorite kind—discontinued. Her purse lay on the dusty floorboard. Maybe when it was all over she could pick up her things. Maybe the bus driver would hold them for her.

Maybe she'd no longer need them.

Her breath hitched as she was led to the road. Her captor gripped her arm, keeping a watchful eye on the bus. The other man disappeared from view. Moments later, a black van skidded to a halt, and the side door popped open.

"Your chariot, pet."

Just before they shoved her inside, she glanced back at the bus. Something crashed against her head.

Then everything went black.

* * *

Cole strained his ears but couldn't hear over the rumbling engine and crying passengers. Had the gunmen left on foot or in a getaway car?

The crying grew louder. One man raised his voice, shaky with fear. "Don't move. Don't want nobody hurt. They said five minutes. Still got four left."

Cole ignored the timekeeper, inching his head up high enough so he could see out the window. The street appeared empty except for a black van. It disappeared around the corner before he could get the license number. He felt under the seat for his belongings. The book was there. His cell phone, gone. They needed to get help fast, get the Atlanta PD looking for that vehicle before Moni—no, the girl from the bench— wound up dead.

Cole half stood, then jerked his gaze to the side as the old man gasped. His hands clutched his chest, and his mouth hung open as sweat trickled down the side of his face.

"Anyone still have a phone?" Cole yelled, leaping to his feet. "This man's having a heart attack!"

"Are you crazy?" the shaky voice yelled again. "Sit down before you get us all killed!"

A woman rose from the last seat and strode forward as the old man's head slumped against the window. "I'm an LPN."

"Good." Cole shoved her into his seat. "Someone help her." He ran up the aisle, but another man beat him to the driver's radio. Cole stared out the windshield. The van was long gone.

"The radio's busted," the man said. "And they took the keys."

"All right. Let's go."

The timekeeper raised his voice from halfway back. "Still got two minutes left, man. You go, you kill that girl."

Cole stiffened, trying to block the image of the girl's face—her sad eyes, her lips white with fear. *If her car hadn't died that morning...* "I stay, and this man dies."

Sirens blared. First a patrol car, then a fire truck, with an ambulance not far behind. Cole blew out a breath, glanced down the aisle where the nurse still hovered. It was out of his hands now. He could tell his story and go. The Atlanta Police Department and emergency response teams would take care of everything.

When the first policeman stepped from the car, the subdued silence on the bus gave way to controlled chaos. In a blur of movement, paramedics whisked the heart attack victim away, the bus was emptied and roped off and a staging area was set up farther down the blocked-off section of street.

Cole sat on the curb and mulled over his statement as emergency personnel began weaving through the crowd, treating injuries and checking those with medical conditions. He played the scene in his head, his pen flying over the paper as he jotted down what had happened, filling in as many details as he could remember.

Two men with black ski masks—he hadn't noticed their faces before the masks went on. Probably should have, because one had been seated right behind him. He should have known, somehow. Should have been able to—

Clenching the pencil tighter, he continued to write. The gun. The boots. Their clothes. The black van. James's heart attack. The search for a phone...

And that was it. Cole sketched the boots and the little he had seen of the men's faces, then turned and stared at the bus. All he'd wanted to do was get a little air and some lunch, kill some time while his cousin was at work. Try to find a little peace between jobs.

He'd found a nightmare instead.

* * *

Thump-thump.

The sounds faded in and out around Kenzie as she regained consciousness: The hum of an engine. The slow-speed, lower-pitched men's voices. The sharp pounding of her heart and the rasping of her own breath.

Thump-thump.

Her head throbbed. She tried to lift a hand to feel for a bruise or gash but couldn't. Something cut into her wrists, binding them behind her back, her fingertips brushing the wall of the vehicle. Her ankles were bound, as well. She tried to force open her eyes, but the blackness stayed.

Thump-thump. Thump-thump.

The walls closed in on her as time stood still in the cloying darkness, dragging her down.

She swallowed hard and shook her head. Not now. Not here. If she didn't want to end up dead, she had to get a grip.

Deep breath. And again.

The walls backed away slightly. Were they going to let her go, like they promised? Or just kill her once they made good on their getaway? She needed to know. But more than that, she needed to be able to see.

Now.

The need for light grew as Kenzie pulled her legs in close and pressed her face against her knee. She rubbed hard, frantically trying to dislodge the blindfold. It stayed, the material cutting into her head, making the ache worse. Pressing her mouth against her knee, Kenzie muffled a whimper.

Then screamed as a hand touched the back of her neck.

THREE

Someone could be dying right now. And here he stood, watching as a crew removed the crime-scene tape from the bus, waiting to be interviewed by a detective as the group anxiously reclaimed their belongings now that they'd been released.

Cole slowly—guiltily—collected his things. His wallet. The novel.

His chest tightened again.

A stylish black purse, the one that the pretty brunette had hugged to herself, remained on the table. Would she ever get it back?

Turning away, he found a spot on the curb again. He needed to call his cousin. See if John could pick him up after his turn with the detective.

Why? So he could go back to his vacation like normal? To act as if he hadn't just watched an innocent woman be marched away, probably to her death…and done nothing about it?

He kept seeing the first paragraph from the Warren Flint book. The words would scroll across his brain, followed by the corresponding actions. The gray seats. The curve in the road. Every second, from watching Monique's twin sit in the front to when the gunmen had hauled her away.

And especially the moment cold metal had touched his temple.

It could have been him…but it wasn't.

When his turn in the hot seat was finished, Cole rose from the metal folding chair and shook hands with the detective. With his interview over, he could go, but…

He should mention the book—just get it out there and let the cops go ahead and discard the notion that it was more than a coincidence. Because then he could, too.

Cole hesitated, then said, "What's the best way to stay up-to-date on the situation?"

Coward. Like they were going to give him inside information.

Detective Parker tipped his bald head and studied Cole through narrowed eyes. "Do you know the hostage?"

"No, sir. I just want to know that she's all right. Makes me feel guilty, you know?" Cole's grip tightened on his belongings.

Detective Parker nodded, his eyes clearing. "I understand, son. But you'll just have to check the news like everyone else."

"Right. Thank you, sir."

As he walked away, the book felt heavy, as if it had taken on his burden of guilt. He sat near the street and balanced the novel on his knee while he waited for his ride. Skimming the pages, he found where he'd left off…where Monique had been taken off the bus. A gun to her head. Shoved in a van. Tied up, blindfolded and whisked away.

He was almost afraid to read the words, almost afraid he'd somehow caused them—as if his imagination typed out each paragraph onto a blank page just before his eyes could catch up. And as if everything on the page was coming to pass.

Right.

It was ridiculous. Crazy. But…what if, by some one-in-a-million chance, the gunmen were using the novel as a playbook for their crime spree?

Then, if he read more and found out what happened to the heroine…there was a one-in-a-million chance he could help save a life.

Monique flexed one hand, then the other. No give in the restraints, but she tried again anyway. She should be wearing the diamond bracelet Evan had given her, not the rope chafing her wrists. Looking through a wispy veil, not sporting a rag blindfold.

She rested her forehead on her knees, just for a moment. Then a sharp turn landed her on her side on the floor of the van. Refusing to cry out, she bit her lip and tasted blood.

"This is your stop, sweetheart." The voice hovered too close above her head and was followed by a sharp jab to her left ankle, then a million needles as blood rushed to her feet. They'd cut the ropes. She should lash out—

A rough hand grabbed her arm, hauled her up. The door opened with a low rumble, and Monique lurched to the ground. Her foot turned on the uneven pavement, and she went down hard. The tears came then, but she forced them back before her captor jerked her upright.

She should be slipping into her borrowed Vera Wang dress, not putting holes in the knees of her designer jeans. She should be kissing Evan, not spitting out dirt and pebbles.

They moved forward, and the way grew more rough. Monique counted each step, tried to remember any turns in the path. Fifteen steps straight ahead. Ten to

*the left. Three more, and she heard a metallic pop. The
sound of a car trunk opening.*

*She should be riding in a car with tin cans rattling
behind it. Not squashed into a trunk like leftover
wedding balloons.*

The hand let go of her arm.

She ran.

Well…at least Monique got away. Maybe this hostage had,
too, and was holed up somewhere hiding out until she felt safe
enough to come home.

Yeah, he could keep telling himself that.

Skimming the page, Cole found his place. Monique fell,
the bad guy caught her and slammed something against her
head. She heard the sound of the trunk lid closing just before
she blacked out.

He could have gone without reading that.

Kenzie huddled in the empty van, the stillness more fright-
ening than being helpless through wild curves and sudden
stops. Once again, she scraped her face against her knee,
trying to work the blindfold up. It shifted, but not enough.

Why did they go away? Did she dare hope they'd left her
for the police to find? Or…did they have something else in
mind? Some further torment or darker ending.

Please, no. Kenzie leaned to the side until she touched the
floor. Dirt clung to her skin, but it didn't matter. She curled
into a tight ball, trying to block out this world, imagine one
of light and fluffy clouds and frothy waves. But instead of
ocean breezes, the air stood still, growing hotter in the closed
vehicle. Sweat trickled down her face, flattening her hair and
stinging her eyes.

Maybe this was part of the plan. Leave her in the dark to

lose her mind, or to succumb to the heat and the pounding pain in her head.

God, if You get me out of this, I'll...

What? What exactly would she do? Buy Him an ice-cream cone, like she'd promised the winner of her class's first-grade spelling bee?

Kenzie flexed her hands, pulling on the ropes. Her wrists ached. She worked them back and forth in an attempt to make the ropes give. No luck. But this was a work van—there must be something in here she could use to cut the ropes. Kenzie bit her lip, trying not to think about her brother's knife, lying abandoned on the bus floor. It would have come in handy about now.

Her fingers scrabbled around the floor. Nothing but dirt. Pushing off with her feet, she moved a couple inches and tried again, until finally her thumb scraped against a jagged scrap of metal. She sucked in a sharp breath at the sting as blood ran down her wrist.

She'd found a way out.

Maybe.

Carefully, Kenzie sat up, adjusted her hands over the metal, brought her wrist down—

A door opened, its hinges screeching out a warning. She took a quick breath, gingerly wrapped her fingers around the makeshift blade, then waited, not having to feign the fearful trembling that seized her limbs.

"Well, pet." The van rocked slightly as someone climbed into the driver's seat. "Time for act one, scene two." He had a slight accent, the hint of an island lilt softening his crisp pronunciation. The gentle inflections and soothing tones should have comforted her. Instead, it raised goose bumps on her arms.

His door slammed, then another opened and closed. As

they pulled back into light, she felt someone's gaze on her, the heat of it scorching her skin. Kenzie hid her face between her knees. If they could just forget about her long enough for her to work on the ropes...

The blood from her cut made the metal sticky. Sweat drenched her blindfold, the back of her black jeans. Fear dried out her mouth so much she couldn't remember if they'd gagged her or if the cotton balls soaking up every drop of saliva were a figment of her dehydrated imagination.

"She's good," the second guy from the bus said.

"Mmm."

"I mean, look at her shaking."

Kenzie tried to still her tremors, but knowing he continued to watch made them grow stronger. What did they want? Why couldn't they just let her go?

"Is she someone I should know?"

"Not yet," the other man answered.

The van slowed to a stop, the engine roughly idling. Heavy feet thudded against the floor. Kenzie refused to lift her head. Instead, she frantically worked the jagged metal against her bindings.

Closer.

Her fingers cramped. She passed the metal to the other hand and worked harder. The van started up again, and the man lurched, his foot hitting close enough beside her that she felt the vibration.

"Hey, was she supposed to have a piece of metal?"

"What?"

Kenzie froze. The man leaned over her—she smelled his body odor. Foul, like his language. His fingers touched hers. Before she could react, her weapon became his.

"Check this out." A pause. "Was she supposed to have this?"

"No." The word was clipped.

Kenzie braced her feet as they rounded a corner, kept her face down, expecting another blow at any moment. Almost welcoming it. If she was unconscious, she wouldn't feel the intense pressure to come up with another escape plan...and fail.

"She's improvising," the redneck said, a note of awe in his voice. Then, to the driver, "Can I keep this?"

The piece of metal. Covered with her blood. A sob caught in her throat. She choked it back. Maybe his little souvenir would lead to his conviction.

After they found her dead.

FOUR

Cole's mouth was dry. He straightened his legs and looked up at the sky. The pages were getting hard to read as the sky turned gray and purple, with a tinge of orange on the horizon. It would be dark soon.

"Cole!" A worried-looking John Brennan stood waving behind the police barricade. "You ready to go, man?"

Cole stepped forward, then caught sight of the detective. The urgency rose up once again. Signaling for his cousin to wait, he called out, "Detective Parker."

His hands grew sweaty as the man changed directions. Too late to back out now.

"Mr. Leighton. You have some more information?" The officer's voice remained gruff, but Cole thought he heard a hint of hope. Or was it annoyance at being disturbed? Probably the former. The annoyance would come after Parker heard what he had to say.

"Just a theory, sir." Another deep breath. "I think the gunmen could be acting out the plot of a novel. *Obsession* by Warren Flint." It sounded even more foolish out loud than it did in his head, and he had to force himself to maintain eye contact. "What if the robbery wasn't their main purpose for being there—the girl was? I had just started reading the book when I got on the bus, and it was like Flint was there with us, writing down everything he saw." Gray seats, two gunmen, one hostage from the front…who looked just like the cover model.

"Maybe the bus scenario was just a coincidence—maybe that's where the similarities will end," Cole said. "But…I don't believe in coincidences. So I read farther, and in the book the heroine was taken hostage and dumped in a boathouse. It's just a crazy idea, but…what if that's where they hid her?"

Parker stared him down before saying, "Mr. Leighton, how about we talk more about this at the station. Do you need a ride?"

He willed away the mental image of being driven, handcuffed, to some psychiatric ward. Wouldn't that look good on his résumé…. "No. Thanks." He gestured toward John. "My cousin just got here."

"Fine. I'm about to wrap up here. Why don't you follow me in?"

Cole gave a short nod.

"I'll be waiting. Hopefully this whole mess will be resolved soon." Parker smiled, and in that smile was just a hint of wolf.

Cole walked toward John under Parker's gaze. Maybe they'd listen. Maybe they'd be so desperate for a lead—any lead—that they'd check it out, just in case.

Or maybe they'd interview him for hours, check out everything, from his last job to his kindergarten report cards, and the hostage would die of hypothermia.

Cole jabbed his fingers into his hair, squeezed, then let go. He could be off his rocker. He could be right on. Either way, those boathouses were going to be checked. Tonight. He'd make sure of it.

* * *

Cold.

Wet.

Dark. So very dark.

Kenzie forced her eyes open, but the darkness remained, taking her breath away. She was surrounded by murky blackness below—the water lapping against her collarbone as her arms stretched up into the shadows. A whimper of fear slipped out, echoing back to her. She squeezed her eyes shut. Took a shuddering breath. Pain. Her head pulsed with it. Her arms, too. Her fingers… Had she fallen? Gotten trapped in a storm?

Where was her brother Mikey?

It came back, too suddenly. The devastating images from her ordeal, then from the past, rushed through her mind like the tornado from that day so long ago. Her brother was dead. And once again she was alone in a storm. She felt lost in the remnants of her past where darkness hovered, its thickness a cold blanket. She gulped in air as fast as she could, but it didn't make it to her lungs. She was drowning…

No. Hyperventilating. Kenzie's eyes slammed shut as her memory came back in a flood. She couldn't do this in the inky blackness—couldn't stay calm, couldn't even think about anything but how dark it was.

Steady. Take it slow. If she could concentrate on her surroundings, maybe she could figure a way out of here. If she couldn't—

She could. Concentrate.

They'd taken off her blindfold. Not that she could see much, but it was something, at least. Rope burned her wrists. They'd lashed her to something—metal chilled her fingertips. If she could get a grip on it, maybe she could pull herself up.

Her sore fingers flexed, then slid down the square bar. She couldn't grip it, not the way her hands were tied together. She curled her hands around the rope instead. One. Two. *Three*. She pulled with her arms, kicked off with her legs. The water swirled around her navel for an instant, then back around her shoulders as she dropped with a grunt. Shivering, she stared upward, seeing the dim outline of the rope and her hands, then the outline of a small boat.

The metal was a lift. They'd dumped her in a boathouse. Why? It didn't matter. Right now her biggest enemy was the water. It couldn't be very deep, but how long had she been in it? Her clothing was soaked through, her arms ached and her body trembled. She had to get out. Had to get warm. Had to find a light.

She needed to do a chin-up. Hold steady. Fling her legs up and out till they hit the deck. Try to propel herself forward enough to hold her body above water. And then what?

She'd cross that bridge when she came to it. *If* she came to it. First she had to get her feet out of the water. A gust of wind rattled the windows, shaking her resolve. What if the water rose or a tornado ripped through?

The tremors grew stronger as she pressed her face into her extended arms, trying to block the sudden images—the ones that always came out along with storms and darkness. The one where she was trapped in the dark listening to the house turn to kindling, waiting in vain for her brother to come back for her.

She wouldn't go there. Couldn't, or she'd be dead. How long did it take for hypothermia to set in? It was a warm spring, but the water was still cold. So cold…

She had to get out of the water. Now.

She tightened her grip on the rope, breathed in and strained to lift her body clear of the water. Up. Up. Hold. One foot hit the underside of the deck, and she sank back down. Biting her lip against the explosion of pain in her ankle, Kenzie tried again. And again and again. The ropes cut deeper into her wrists. Her legs banged against wood and scraped against metal until tears flowed freely down her face. She couldn't quit, but her arms were on fire. Her legs barely cleared the water.

Breathe in. Breathe out.

Kenzie closed her eyes, envisioning each move. Maybe if she saw herself doing it, she'd believe it, and, believing, it would happen.

Sure. Then why didn't she just "see" a rescuer burst through the door? Or maybe God's hand gently scooping her up and transporting her back to her couch at home? When had believing ever worked for her?

A low rumble of thunder, then another, closer. Kenzie tried to swallow. Couldn't. Her mouth tasted metallic. *God, I don't want to die here. In a storm, in the dark…like Mikey.*

Maybe that's why this was happening. Her punishment for putting her brother in danger. For letting him die in her place. He was the darling child, after all. The beloved son.

She opened her eyes and caught a fleeting image. Mikey. Staring at her—his own eyes unseeing and lifeless. No, just a hallucination, but still the scream came, catching in her throat, then pushing its way through. Loud, long. Ending in a gasping sob. She screamed again. Wind rattled the walls, but no one came. Another scream.

But no one heard.

FIVE

"This is unreal, man," John said as Cole slid into the truck. "I didn't think they were going to let you go."

Cole caught his cousin's sidelong glance, and his face heated. "I didn't think you'd come back after what I told you on the way in."

"It's weird, but I believe you. I think. Did the police?"

Cole shut out the memory of the officer's steely eyes. "No. But Parker couldn't come up with any reason to hold me." But he would in a couple of hours... "Did you bring your gun?"

John pointed to the glove compartment.

Cole opened it and tugged out a map, a knife then the Glock. The cool feel of it soothed him as John pulled the truck onto the road.

"Should we get some coffee to go?"

"There's no 'we,'" Cole said.

"If you're doing this, I'm doing this, okay? What good is family if they won't go out for an evening of boathouse hopping with you? Besides, I'm the one with a license to carry that beauty." John grinned, then sobered. "You really think she's there?"

"No... Yes." He closed his eyes. "I have no idea. But I sat on that bus and did absolutely nothing while they took her. If

I go back home and wake up tomorrow to find out my bizarre theory was right…"

"Okay, man. Then let's do this. You said we're looking for a small lake near a larger one. Secluded. Affluent-community type thing, correct?"

"Exactly." Cole had studied that chapter of the book, read it over and over again, gleaned as many details as he could. "In *Obsession*, it seems like they drove maybe an hour. So…"

"So we're looking for something that's an hour away, right?"

"Or less. Right." Maybe.

John shoved the map toward Cole and edged the Dodge Ram back onto the road. "I'll head up I-85. There's an area near Lake Lanier kind of like you're talking about. Some of Kasey's clients live up there. Nice homes."

"And what would your girlfriend say if she knew what I was dragging you into?" They could get arrested, maybe worse if someone decided to try out their shotgun collection on intruders.

"We're just friends. And…she'd wonder why she wasn't invited." John smiled. "So let's do this. But if the girl isn't right there—" John pointed to the map. "I don't know where else to look."

"As long as we do what we can." Cole glanced up as lightning sliced through the night sky.

So…c-cold.

Rain hit the roof, a solid wall of sound. Occasional crackles of lightning lit the boathouse, making the shadows deeper while spotlighting the boat, the lift, the lack of color in her hands.

An eerie keening filled the room, echoing off the walls. It wasn't until the lapping water choked it off that she realized it came from her own throat.

She was going to die here.

No! She'd get through this. Maybe she could work the knots loose. Bite through them. Rub them against a bolt on the lift until she could break free. Awkwardly, Kenzie ran her icy fingers along the couple inches of metal she could reach. Smooth. Maybe she could slide down just a little. There had to be some sort of screw or…or something. Had to. She couldn't just hang here. Willing strength into her legs, she kicked against the water. Nothing. Again, with more force this time. Still nothing, and she was tiring fast.

"God!" Her cry reverberated back to her. She doubted He heard. No one could hear over this storm. No one would be coming to her rescue. If she wanted to live, she had to work. Had to come up with some other plan. There had to be some way…

But not right now. After she'd rested a bit. S-so tired…

Kenzie relaxed her head against her arm, allowed her eyes to drift closed. That felt a little better. A little warmer. A little more—

Her chin hit the water and she jerked her head back up, heart pounding so loud she could hear it thudding in her ears. If she slept, she died.

Trespassing. Breaking and entering. What other laws would they break tonight? Though they hadn't actually broken anything and weren't planning on robbing anyone, Cole doubted good intentions would win them any favors if they were caught creeping around a stranger's boathouse.

Of course, the real question was, what would it do to his job search if anyone found out about his crazy Lone Ranger crime spree?

"Nothing?" John whispered as Cole stepped away from the boathouse.

Cole shook his head, and they jogged back to the truck.

"How many more on this lake?" The rain had soaked through Cole's clothing, chilling his skin. And they'd only been outside for a few minutes at each stop. How long had the hostage been in the water?

If this wasn't all in his head.

"I think two more. Maybe three."

So they'd check two or three more. Then they'd go home, John would get a laugh, and Cole would get a shower. He'd check the news a couple times, throw the book away, wash his hands of the whole thing…and begin an intensive search for his sanity.

"Here's the next one."

Cole peered through the swishing windshield wipers, but without the headlights on, everything was shadow. Taking a deep breath, he nodded. With John just behind him, he jumped out of the truck, ducking as rain blurred his view, and ran, sticking to the cover of the trees. The dark outline of a boat-house loomed in front of him, but he stopped behind a tree and studied it first as John came up behind him.

Lightning flared, illuminating a cabin off to the right. No lights. No vehicles. Even so, his steps slowed as he neared the lake. John stayed back, his gun in hand as he kept watch. Stopping under the boathouse's overhang, Cole peered into a window. His breath fogged the already-cloudy glass. Too dark.

The door stood a few yards away. Cole gripped the handle; it turned easily, but the door creaked as it opened. The rain on the roof roared loudly enough to cover the sound. Still no movement. Number three—another waste of time. But he stepped inside to double-check. If she was here, she might be unconscious.

Or dead.

No one on the deck to the right. He moved to the left, walking softly as he searched the shadows. All clear.

The rain let up for a moment—a light patter on tin—and he heard something. A soft whine. No, a sob. The voice faded into a whimper as lightning flared.

A woman in the water. Hands tied to the lift. Hair floating around her shoulders.

He fumbled for the light switch as she slowly turned toward him, her eyes dark hollows in a face pale as death. "Help…m-me." Her soft voice trembled almost as much as her body, but she was still conscious, still alive.

If he could just keep her that way until help arrived.

"My name is Cole Leighton. We met earlier today." He kept his voice low and steady, trying to stay calm as he strode to the doorway. "You're going to be fine."

Cole hollered for John and edged closer to the water. The light shone on the lift and her ropes, then her blue-tinged fingers. Wincing, he threw off his jacket while he kept up a one-sided conversation.

"My cousin John is calling nine-one-one. I'm going to get you out of the water and get you warm, okay? You'll be fine. Help is on the way."

He searched his pockets for the knife he'd taken from the glove compartment. There. He slipped into the cold water, and it hit him mid-chest.

"What's your name?" he asked as he waded to her.

"M-MacKenzie Jacobs." Her answer was barely above a whisper as he cautiously hooked an arm around her waist. The rope held her up too far—her feet didn't quite touch bottom.

"Okay, MacKenzie. I'm just going to keep my arm around you so you don't sink when I cut the rope, okay? Then you'll be out of here." He held her carefully, feeling her violent tremors against his chest. How long had they left her out here? The heat of his anger should warm her in seconds.

Cole sawed at the thick rope, watching the strands give way. Too slowly. "Come on, come on, come *on*."

The door flew open. MacKenzie didn't respond. Just stayed with her head resting against his shoulder, shivering uncontrollably.

SIX

"Cops are on the way." A new voice.

Kenzie didn't want to move. Just wanted to sleep, to curl up against this wall of warmth, with the strong arm holding her, the steady voice in her ear, the light shining on her. Just wanted to float away...

"What can I do?"

She blinked as that other voice spoke again, but let her eyes drift shut. Please be quiet. Please, please...

"Help me get her out of here. Into the truck."

She felt the rumble of the first, familiar voice. The voice that brought the light. Then the pressure was off her arms. Her hands dropped, splashing water into her face. She didn't react. Couldn't.

"MacKenzie? Still with me?"

Another arm scooped up her legs—she barely felt it, but then she was cuddled closer to that warm wall. The water swirled around her calves. She couldn't feel her feet. Other hands touched her arms. Tried to pull her away—no. No!

"She doesn't want you to let go, Cole."

"It's all right, MacKenzie. John's a friend."

No. She wanted to stay there. Just stay...

"Is the heat running?" The first voice, farther away. She couldn't feel the vibrations of his voice, the pounding of his heart. Don't leave…

"Yeah. Here, you got her?"

"Try not to jostle her."

Snuggled close again. Something warm over her knees, her head.

"MacKenzie, talk to me, girl. Keep those pretty eyes open."

"Still got the dispatcher on the phone."

A sprinkling of water, then a blast of hot air. So hot. The lightning—must be burning her up.

"Good. How long…"

The words faded in and out. Kenzie tried to keep listening, but then just the tone was enough. The first voice was there. Still soothing, even though she burned like fire.

"MacKenzie?"

She tried to answer. Bright lights filled her vision, then she faded away.

The police and paramedics had arrived just as Cole removed one of MacKenzie's waterlogged shoes. From inside the truck, he now watched as she disappeared behind the ambulance doors, following the flashing lights with his gaze as it sped out of view. It was over. He'd been right.

Now he just hoped he hadn't been too late.

"So now what?" His spiky hair mussed and dripping, John loosely held the steering wheel and stared at the rain.

"Now…" He pictured MacKenzie's shoeless right foot. *Please, God, let her be okay.*

Detective Parker tapped on his window. Cole hit the unlock button and waited as the officer climbed into the backseat, the suspicion in his face making Cole's blood freeze.

"It seems you were right, Cole Leighton."

"Yes, sir." Cole closed his eyes, then opened them and stared straight ahead. He could use a blanket of his own right now.

"We did a sweep of the area—no one was here except you guys. We can't do much in this rain. CSI has it covered for now, so why don't you two come back to the station and give us your statements? There are a few things we need to clear up."

"That's fine." Actually, it wasn't, but he doubted he had a choice.

"Mind if we get into some dry clothes first?" John asked.

Cole caught his cousin's sideways look. The heat blasted the outside of his jeans, but they were still wet and stiff. Water squished between his toes, which reminded him again of MacKenzie's blue foot.

"Oh, it shouldn't take too long. We've got some blankets. Coffee. Let's get it over with, in case there's some pertinent information."

John nodded his reluctant agreement.

"Good," Parker said. "I'll follow you there."

The door opened, and rain rushed in before it slammed shut. Parker got out and the detective faded behind sheets of rain. They waited in silence until Parker's car flashed its high beams. John put the Dodge in gear and headed for the main road.

When they hit pavement, John said, "How come I get the feeling this interview is going to be more like an interrogation?"

"I'm sorry, John."

"No, man. You did the right thing. I'm just saying…they better have some good coffee."

Cole forced a laugh. "Don't count on it. But maybe they put on a new pot since I was there last." Less than two hours ago. Parker's eyes had narrowed then. This time they'd be mere slits. He wouldn't try to figure out if Cole was a kook or a paranoid bookworm or a bad guy. He'd be pretty certain of the latter. A bad guy with a hero complex.

Well, he'd be basically correct, wouldn't he?

"Cole, you did the right thing," John said again. "You have an alibi. There's no way they're going to believe you did this."

In spite of the chill, a bead of sweat dripped down his face. Not good. They'd probably take his fear as an indication of guilt, a sign that he knew something.

"What are the odds?" he said. "Only a few days in town and I just happened to choose that bus, that book, at that time? And I didn't have anything to do with it?" One in a million. One in a hundred million. No, more like…zero, zilch. No chance at all.

"Tell me." John's face was hard, his eyes on the road. "Did you have anything to do with it?"

Cole flinched. "No."

"I didn't think so. The odds aren't good—so what? Maybe God stuck you on that bus at that time with that book and gave you the wisdom to figure things out. Because He knows how stubborn you can be." John glanced away from the windshield, caught Cole's gaze, then concentrated on the road again. "You saved the girl's life. We can deal with whatever happens next."

Cole swallowed. Closed his eyes. He'd felt, for that brief moment when he'd held MacKenzie Jacobs—when he lifted her from the water and set her carefully in the backseat of the truck—that he could redeem himself. That this life could make up for one that was lost years ago. That he could start over again with a fresh page in God's book.

But that would have been too easy, and he deserved anything but easy.

Cole folded his arms on the tabletop and lowered his head. At three in the morning, he didn't really care if the action might seem suspicious. His heavy eyelids refused to stay open. So, while he waited for Parker to return, he'd take advantage of the reprieve.

His aching eyes closed, but his mind would not shut down. The routine rolled through his mind—he'd been through it before. They'd analyze the recording of his interview. Maybe test the stress levels in his voice for indications of guilt. There would be stress, all right—he'd been stressed out for almost twenty-four hours. More like twenty-four years, but that was beside the point.

Shut up, Cole.

A chair scraped, jerking him to awareness once again. Lifting his head, he found Parker sitting across from him.

"Sorry to keep you up so late, Mr. Leighton," he said in a neutral tone. "Just a couple more things and then we'll let you go get some much deserved rest."

"Go ahead."

"We'd like you to take a polygraph test. That'll really help us wrap a few things up, and then we won't need to take much more of your time."

At least, not after they'd locked him up and thrown away the key.

"Fine." As if he had a choice.

"Good." Parker smiled. "Secondly, I wondered if you'd loan us your copy of that book."

Cole gave a brief nod. "I'd be glad to." Parker shouldn't need a polygraph to hear the truth ringing in that statement.

Kenzie didn't want to open her eyes. The warm bed and soft hospital pillow called to her. Last night she thought she'd never be comfortable again. Now she was, and she didn't want to move. Ever.

Then the aches hit. Her head. Her hands and wrists and legs. Everywhere, she hurt.

"MacKenzie?"

"Mmm," she said, not opening her eyes. She didn't want to find out if they hurt, too.

"Oh, honey…"

"Mom." Her lips were cracked. "You missed your flight. You didn't need to come." The days of needing her mother were past…and Mom hadn't been there then, anyway.

"Oh, it was no bother. Somebody needs to take care of your houseplants until you come home." She spoke in overly bright tones this time, and it was almost worse than when her voice had dripped with pity. "Did you see the flowers someone sent you? Beautiful roses for a beautiful girl."

Ah, yes. There was the pity again.

Her suffering could have been over. Just a little longer in the water, and Kenzie would no longer have to wish she was the one who died and Mikey was the one who lived.

Kenzie finally opened her eyes to stare at the roses, not allowing herself to glimpse her mother's expression. She'd learned to read her well, but at this moment she didn't want to know what lay between the lines in her mother's furrowed brow.

"Is there a card?"

Her mother's graceful fingers stretched toward the vase and rotated it. "Nothing."

"Did you...see who brought them?" The man who'd saved her? She held her breath, hoping she hadn't missed him, yet hoping he had come.

"They were here when I arrived."

"Mmm." Kenzie turned her face toward the ceiling and blinked as the tiles swam out of focus.

"Are you okay? Anything I can do for you?"

"I'm fine. Thanks. Just need sleep." The blankets weighed her down until they smothered the incessant beeping and the aching pain.

Someone rapped on the door, then cracked it open.

Kenzie held her breath, fighting the urge to run. No one would hurt her here. The kidnappers had made their escape. That's all they'd wanted, right?

But she closed her fingers around the television remote—some weapon—and slowly turned her head. A police officer stood just inside the doorway, his expression grim and tired.

"Miss Jacobs?"

"Yes." Letting go of the remote, Kenzie drew her blankets close, then adjusted her bed until she was sitting up.

"I'm Detective Parker. Mind if I ask you a few questions?"

She was too tired to dredge up yesterday's nightmare, but, pasting on a smile, Kenzie nodded.

The policeman came around the bed and opened the blinds slightly, then scooted a chair close. Out of his briefcase came a black folder with a legal pad, a bulky pen, a digital recorder.

Her eyes drifted closed, exhausted by the mere sight of his equipment.

"Miss Jacobs." The detective's kind voice pulled her from the edge of sleep. "I don't want to put off this interview since the more we know, the more likely we are to make arrests. But if you're not up to it..."

"No, please. Wouldn't want to hold up justice." She meant it, but her eyelids did not want to cooperate.

Finally they fluttered open, and she found the man settling into his chair, legs crossed and folder propped just so. He'd done this before. Caught lots of criminals. If she could just stay awake, she could help him catch more. Then this whole thing would be over and life could get back to normal. Whatever that was.

Maybe now she'd have something new to mix in with her old nightmares. She still felt the gun against her temple, the rope chafing her wrists, the water lapping around her shoulders. Maybe because she relived it every time her eyes closed.

Detective Parker cleared his throat. "Miss Jacobs, I want you to run through everything that happened yesterday, but first, can you describe the men who took you?"

"No." From now until the moment the camo guy and his smooth-accented boss landed behind bars, she'd probably suspect every male who came within twenty feet of her.

As if her dating life wasn't bad enough already.

"I was blindfolded most of the time, but…" She allowed her eyes to close again, brought up the image of the bus and talked about what she'd seen, felt, heard. She told him about the leather jacket and sinewy arm locked around her shoulders. The ski mask and how that, almost more than the gun, gave the man a twisted and terrifying appearance. She hadn't noticed his eye color; the glint of metal had been a stronger draw for her gaze.

"There were two men." A shudder shifted the blanket. Kenzie clenched it in her fists, chilled once again. "The man with the camouflage jacket must have driven the van away, while the man with the leather jacket took me to…to the boathouse. But everything's kind of hazy. I blacked out when they put me in the trunk of a car, and when I woke up, I was in the water. That…that's all. I'm sorry."

"You're doing fine. Do you think—"

"Wait…" She paused with her eyes tightly closed. Remembering. Shadows filled her mind. A blur of black and gray and white-hot pain. "At the boathouse, I think I came to for a moment when the man with the accent took off my blindfold. Just before he—" She choked back an unexpected sob.

"Take your time, Miss Jacobs."

A gulping breath. Warm air filled her lungs, and she found the strength to focus again on the vague memory. "So dark, but he must have had a flashlight. I saw…"

She was flopped over his knee, one of his arms steadying her while his other pulled the blindfold free. Legs untied, wrists bound more tightly, but in front of her now.

Her breath came faster. She was falling. Knees hit the deck hard. Turned her head as her hands—forced out over the water—touched metal. Caught a glimpse of dark hair, lighter neck, white scar.

Then she plunged into the icy water.

A quick gasp. No. She was okay now. But the tremors took over again. And, as she tried to recount the day through chattering teeth—every exhausting and excruciating detail—she wondered if she'd ever really feel safe again.

SEVEN

Cole stopped at the end of the corridor and stared at the number on MacKenzie's hospital room. He fingered the get-well card, wishing he'd thought to purchase flowers, as well. Maybe he should go to the gift shop—

Too late. The door swung open. Detective Parker stepped out.

Cole stood tall, not bothering to force a smile.

"She's pretty tired," the detective finally said, his steely eyes giving a silent warning.

Cole didn't flinch. "I won't be long."

"Good." Parker gave him a pointed look. "She's been through a lot."

Time for that fake smile. "That's why I'm here."

A short nod, and the detective finally walked away— probably no farther than a vacant chair in the hall. Cole took a breath, then stepped into the room, leaving the door partially open behind him. He had nothing to hide. Mac-Kenzie lay silent, her eyes closed. He should leave, let her rest undisturbed, but his feet remained planted to the floor at the foot of her bed. His chest ached as he scanned her for signs of her ordeal—pale skin, a bandage taped to her left temple—

Her eyelids fluttered, then opened. A gasp escaped her chapped lips, stabbing his conscience as her dark-blue eyes widened in shock.

"I'm sorry, MacKenzie." Why had he stayed? Staring at her while she slept... Of all the thoughtless— "I just wanted to drop off a card for you." He set it on the side table and started to back away.

"Kenzie," she said softly. "My friends call me Kenzie." The fear was gone from her face, and her eyes shone when she looked at him.

Kenzie. Casual, but slightly exotic. It fit her well. A real smile stretched his lips as she met his gaze and held it.

"I'm Cole. Don't know if you remember me from the bus stop or...later. But you're going to be okay."

She seemed so fragile, but her nod reassured him. "Thanks to you." Tears gathered in her eyes. "How did you find me?"

The question of the hour. Cole sat down and considered his response. The truth was too out-of-this-world, so Cole settled on a more believable but equally out-of-this-world answer. "Must have been a God thing."

Her tears slipped free, and he glanced away, not wanting to see her cry. His gaze fell on her hands, and without thinking, he gently tugged one toward the edge of the bed and examined it. Ointment covered the raw red burns. Band-Aids hid the smaller wounds but not her bruises.

"Are you in pain?" he asked softly.

"Not too bad. Just tired. How can I ever...?"

He shook his head. "You don't owe me anything. I'm just glad you're going to be all right."

"Mmm." Kenzie's eyes closed briefly. "You think Detective Parker will catch them?"

"Hope so." For more reasons than one. "He's very thorough."

"I'm just glad it's over. Or almost." Her voice softened to a pained whisper. "I thought I wasn't going to make it."

"I know."

Her hand moved until her fingers rested on his palm, a feather-light touch. "When you walked in and turned on the light, I felt safe for the first time in...in a long time."

Cole couldn't find a response.

Her fingers tapped his, then withdrew. "Thank you."

Cole blinked and raised his gaze to her face, but her eyes were shut. "You're welcome," he whispered.

She didn't answer. He fiddled with her controls, lowering the bed to a more comfortable sleeping position. Kenzie's eyes opened slightly, then fell shut again. Sun shone brightly through the open blinds and the warm rays played across her face, disguising her bruises as shadows.

A satchel rested beside his chair. It belonged to someone in her family, no doubt. Someone who would be returning soon and might not welcome company. He started to rise, wanting to stay—to make sure she stayed safe and kept breathing those slow, even breaths—but not wanting to be in the way.

The chair creaked, and Kenzie stirred, then stretched a hand toward him. "Don't...leave," she whispered, eyes still closed.

Cole swallowed the lump in his throat and settled back down, her hand cradled carefully in his as she retreated once again into sleep. Why hadn't he gone looking for her sooner? Talking to Parker had just stalled him. If he'd just allowed himself to trust his instincts, Kenzie may still have been hurt, but he might have been able to shorten her ordeal.

He shook his head once. MacKenzie Jacobs would live to see another day, to light up the world with her smile. He had been late, but not *too* late this time. Her nightmare was over.

Or was it?

Cole froze as he pictured the cover of *Obsession,* the scrap of paper that marked his spot, only a few chapters in when he'd turned it over to the detective.

If Monique's car hadn't died, she might not have either…

He'd only read to the part about the boathouse before reporting to Parker and going on his trespassing frenzy. If Monique's story hadn't ended there…would Kenzie's?

Kenzie opened her eyes to an empty chair and a dark room. Strange shadows shifted, and her heart pounded hard against her ribcage. Where was Cole Leighton and his calming presence? Had he really left her alone?

Then again, why should that surprise her?

She drew in rapid breaths as the darkness seemed to loom closer. Get a grip. There was no storm, no danger, surely no gunmen lurking in the hallways. She was safe.

A shadow moved. Her breath halted altogether as the door creaked open.

"You're awake." The brightness from the hall illuminated her mother's face. "Mind if I turn the light on?"

"Please," Kenzie forced out, choking back tears of relief as light flooded the room once again.

Her mother set a vase of carnations next to the roses and settled into the vacant chair. "You've had a steady stream of visitors this afternoon. I came back from lunch and met that young man—I guess the one who found you? Anyway, I know how you like your privacy—"

Yeah, well, if her mother knew so much about her, why had she shut off the light? Kenzie had been terrified of the dark since she was nine years old. Ever since the night of the tornado that took her brother.

"So I sent him on his way."

Cole Leighton hadn't left her alone after all. Not that it should matter either way—she was indebted to him, not the other way around. But somehow, it did.

"Your principal stopped by. He left these." Her mother indicated the bouquet she'd brought in.

Kenzie reached for the card and slowly exhaled as she read it. She'd been granted sick leave for as long as she needed if she wasn't ready to go back to teaching first grade after spring break.

Detective Parker entered the room and her mother excused herself. Had they found the gunmen? Kenzie forced back the rush of hope, not wanting to feel the crush of it if she was disappointed.

Once more, the police officer sat beside her bed, recorder in hand. "I'm sorry to disturb you again, Miss Jacobs, but I do have just a couple more questions for you." His heavy eyebrows lifted as if awaiting a go-ahead.

She nodded, wondering what else he could have to ask. They'd already been over everything from a dozen different directions, as far as she could tell: Who she'd had contact with before the bus ride. Why she hadn't taken her car. Who her enemies were. Why someone would have targeted her. If the gunmen seemed to have planned the kidnapping…

"Had you ever met Cole Leighton before yesterday? Ever seen him around the school, at church…anything?"

They hadn't covered that. Something inside her tightened, constricting her breath. "No." She would have remembered those eyes, that wistful smile. "I only know that if it weren't for him—" Kenzie blinked, remembering how numb her hands had been, how unresponsive her legs had become by the time help had reached her. "I owe him my life."

Detective Parker made a note to himself, then looked at her again. "And when he visited earlier…"

His eyebrows raised again, and her insides coiled tighter. "He just came to make sure I was going to be okay." She wished she'd gotten to say good-bye, wished her mother hadn't kicked him out. Would she ever see him again?

"Did he bring you anything?"

Her eyes strayed to the roses. "Just a card."

His gaze must have followed hers. "No flowers?"

"I don't think so." Although she could always hope. "What's going on?" She met the detective's keen stare.

"Just covering all the angles." He waited a moment, then stood when she didn't speak again. "Miss Jacobs, we're doing everything we can, following every lead. But I want you to be careful. Any odd phone call or visitor—you let me know about it. Deal?"

"Deal."

After he left, Kenzie pushed the principal's bouquet to the side and caressed the vase holding her first get-well flowers. Seven red roses. She studied the crimson petals, gingerly touched one, and searched again for a card. None.

Had Cole sent them? Maybe he'd forgotten to attach a card and had hand-delivered one instead; he had set it beside the roses, after all. Kenzie tapped a stem, then pulled her hand back to her side. Her arms still ached, her eyelids still drooped. But she'd seen the man who had saved her life, and somehow that made things better. Not just because he was, well, *really* attractive, with his shaggy hair, piercing blue-green eyes and gentle smile. She'd remembered his eyes from before boarding the bus, his voice from when he'd shined a light in her darkness. His quiet strength made her feel safe, but not smothered. He made her feel beautiful, even with chapped lips and hideous wrists and frazzled hair, leaving her with a longing to be loved for who she was.

Except that could never happen—she'd never allow it. Because whenever she truly loved someone, whenever they truly loved her...

They ended up dead.

EIGHT

Cole picked up the bookstore's last copy of *Obsession* and found an empty chair. The overstuffed furniture was comfortable—the reading was anything but. Monique hadn't been rescued as soon as Kenzie had. Her hypothermia had been so severe that her rescuer hadn't found a heartbeat. The medical crew had had to wait until Monique's body was rewarmed before they would decide whether or not to pronounce her dead.

Cole's stomach clenched at the thought that he could have pulled Kenzie's pasty-blue, lifeless body from the water. His phone vibrated, and he reached for it without looking away from the book.

"Cole, have you eaten?" John said.

"No." He glanced at the time. Quarter till seven. "What's up?"

"I'm craving a burger from The Varsity. Been there yet?"

"Nope." The hunger pangs hit then. A juicy hamburger. Fries doused in ketchup. A cold Coke with lots of ice. An hour of food and carefree conversation to help him forget that he'd escaped death. While a passenger from the same bus lay in a hospital bed, eating hospital food, reliving the same nightmare but a hundred times worse.

"It sounds great, but I think I'll take a rain check. I'm

going to run an errand and grab something on the go." Book still in hand, Cole headed for the checkout line.

"Be careful, Cole."

His determined stride faltered slightly at the sober note in his cousin's voice. "Why?"

"Are you going to check on the pretty lady again?"

"Yes."

"Then just…be careful."

The call ended, and Cole stared at the phone for a moment before returning it to its clip. Was John's warning because of the book, because of his past or because of the good detective who was undoubtedly keeping an eye on him for suspicious behavior?

"Awesome book, let me tell you," the cashier said, interrupting his thoughts. She rang up the total, then tapped her long, red nails against the countertop while waiting for Cole's credit card to go through. "By the way!" Her red hair nearly bounced with her enthusiasm as she bagged the novel and shook it in the air. "If you bring this back this coming Thursday, you can have the author autograph it for you!"

Cole followed the ridiculous length of fingernail to where she pointed at a poster for a book signing. Warren Flint. Coming to Atlanta a week after the first scene of his bestselling novel had been played out in real life.

Cole figured his idea of comfort food—steak and eggs with a Texas-size Coke—would differ slightly from a woman's. Especially one who'd nearly frozen to death the day before. Something hot and something chocolate should do the trick. It wouldn't wipe away the traces of her ordeal, of course. Nor would it erase his feelings of guilt. But…if nothing else, it had to be better than hospital Jell-O.

He strode down the hospital corridor and stopped at Kenzie's door. No one stood outside. No voices came from the interior. Fighting down a sudden urgency, Cole forced himself to knock gently.

No answer.

He twisted the knob, and the door glided open on silent hinges. He paused, almost expecting Parker to step into his line of vision and pierce him with a suspicious glare.

No one.

Cole stood in the doorway, watching Kenzie sleep, until he realized his fingers were digging into the bag of food. Her sandwich would have thumb-size gouges in it if he didn't rein in his feelings.

Why had they left her alone?

He moved to the bed, cautiously setting down the food on her tray table. Though the paper bags crinkled and the chair creaked when he settled into it, Kenzie's eyes remained closed. For one blood-chilling moment, he thought she was dead. Her pale face, her dark-shadowed eyelids—but the blanket rose and fell with each breath. Her hands appeared warm and freshly slathered with ointment. Her thick eyelashes fluttered slightly, then lifted until her disoriented gaze met his.

"Hey." He smiled, suddenly feeling like squirming. "Thought you might like something to eat other than hospital food."

Lame. Her mother had probably gotten something for her already. Or maybe his first visit had been more than enough. Maybe MacKenzie Jacobs would rather close the door on yesterday—including him—and move on.

Not that he could blame her. He just apparently had a problem doing the same himself. Why? He suddenly felt like kicking himself. Kenzie wasn't Allison. He needed to let go, stop using her as salve for his guilty conscience.

She smiled and pulled the first bag closer. "It smells wonderful."

Something tight inside loosened as he helped unload the bags. "Tomato-basil soup, chicken and roasted red-pepper *panini* and some sort of chocolate-filled pastry."

Kenzie stared at the pastry, blue eyes sparkling. "Maybe I died after all, because this has got to be pretty close to heaven."

"Let me go grab a drink for you." But suddenly he didn't want to leave, was afraid that if he did, he'd come back to find her dead after all. Cole swallowed the paranoia and forced a smile. "Juice? Water? Soda?"

"Water would be great."

She focused her beautiful smile on him, and then he wanted to stay for an altogether different reason.

Her eyes clouded. "Did Mom say where she was going?"

Cole blinked and cleared his throat. "I must have missed her."

"You didn't see her?"

"No."

Conflicting emotions crossed Kenzie's face. Cole couldn't identify the first—pain, maybe? But the second was unmistakably fear.

"She probably went to grab a bite to eat while you slept." He kept his voice calm, refusing to allow her sudden panic to induce the same in him. Since he was the only one who seemed afraid to leave Kenzie unguarded, maybe that meant he was overreacting after all.

Please, God.

Cole's presence had more to do with the warming of Kenzie's insides than did the hot meal he'd provided. His gentle gaze, his Texas drawl, the way he hovered, ready to help if necessary but not pushing his assistance on her...

The perfect gentleman. He just needed a black cowboy hat to tip in her direction, and he'd be all set.

Careful, Kenzie.

She'd nearly died last night—a terrifying death. Cole Leighton saved her from that. She was allowed to bask in the safety his presence provided, at least for a little while. Then she'd go home, life would go back to normal and she'd banish her hero to dreams of white knights. Once he determined she was truly okay, her knight would go on to save other damsels in distress, forgetting entirely about her. Which was as it should be, even though the thought brought a twinge of regret.

"All done?" Cole asked.

At her nod, he cleared the tray table…which probably meant he was about to leave. She tried to tell herself it didn't matter—visiting hours were almost over anyway. But it *did* matter. And her mom had still not returned.

The fear pricked like an IV needle, and the chill of it crept through her veins.

Cole threw the last of her feast away and met her eyes with a look of steady understanding. "You want me to look for your mom? Or is there a number you can call?"

"Um…" *Mom, where* are *you?*

It hurt how familiar that question was as it echoed through her mind. She'd been asking it for years. Ever since Mikey died…

Kenzie bit her lip, then ran trembling fingers through her messy hair. When she pulled her hand away, several strands stuck to the ointment. What a mess.

The phone rang. Kenzie closed her eyes, almost afraid to reach for it. What if it was the police, informing her of an accident?

Cole answered for her. She listened to his soothing tones, the lack of strain, and her heartbeat calmed as he handed her the phone.

"Mom?"

"MacKenzie, I'm so sorry. While you were napping, I thought I'd run to your place and bring back some things for you. But then I got lost and the traffic is horrendous."

Welcome to Atlanta. "I'm fine." Almost. "I'm just glad you're okay."

"Yes, but I'm upset. I spoke to the nurse, and they won't let me stay with you tonight. Now that you're recovering, visiting hours are limited. And I'm not going to make it there before they lock up. So you're on your own, darling."

Kenzie closed her eyes once again. "All right."

"See you first thing in the morning, MacKenzie. Sleep well."

Unlikely. Kenzie hung up without saying good-bye, but her mother had already beaten her to it.

A few moments later, a voice over the intercom announced the end of visiting hours. Cole met her gaze for a moment, touched her fingertips then moved toward the door and reached for the light.

"Please." She hated the note of desperation that crept into her voice. "Leave it on."

Cole's eyes narrowed, seeing too much, and her gaze flitted to her hands in shame. But when she looked him in the face again, he didn't question her fear. Just nodded and twisted the doorknob.

"Sleep well, Kenzie."

Funny, how the same words from Cole conjured up a different reaction. With Mom, it was just an expression. With Cole, he looked at her as if he knew what monsters would haunt her in the nighttime hours.

Cole lounged on John's couch, wishing he were at the hospital instead. But he could do one thing, at least. Read Warren Flint's book, see if his theory was right and make sure that nothing else bad should happen to Kenzie. He wished he could put the thriller down, but instead hung on every word in morbid fascination.

Monique raised her eyes to a splash of red. She blinked, focused, saw the roses with their open faces, welcoming her back to life. She smiled. Evan... Her eyes drooped closed again. When she found the strength to open them, she carefully shifted her gaze over each flower, counting. In their code, one red rose said, "You are the one." Two, mutual affection. Three, "I love you."

Half a dozen, then one more. Monique pulled the additional stem from the vase and held it to her nose, thinking. Six roses meant he missed her. Seven... Evan had never sent seven roses before. She stared into the heart of the rose, and its message finally came.

Obsession.

Cole set the book down. Flint kept distant from his character's emotions, but Cole could imagine the chill. It was the same one that crept down his back as he tried to remember if there had been roses in Kenzie's hospital room. He vaguely recalled some floral arrangements, but he'd been too focused on her—her wounded hands and gorgeous smile and fear-filled gaze—to notice much else.

Maybe the roses were really from Monique's boyfriend. Nothing to be concerned about. No reason to wonder if Kenzie had received something similar. Maybe Flint had titled the book after the meaning of the flowers.

Or maybe because he'd worked some sort of magic that brought the story to life, pulling readers in until they were the ones obsessed. Whatever it was, Cole lifted the book, and he buried his nose once again.

Evan walked through the door, his handsome face a study of concern. She set the flower on her lap and smiled a greeting. He approached the bed, carrying roses. More than seven. Monique counted slowly as the blooms waved their proud heads. Thirty-three. I love you completely.

Her gaze shifted to the first bouquet, and Evan read her unspoken request. He plucked the card from the roses, opened the envelope, and read it out loud.

Till we meet again.

Cole stared at the words, mouthed them, told himself that it was just a novel. It had nothing whatsoever to do with Kenzie anymore.

Yeah, right.

NINE

Home, sweet home.

"MacKenzie, are you sure you'll be okay?"

Maybe she would be if Mom ever stopped hovering. Kenzie sat in a high-backed chair in her kitchen, avoiding her mother's eyes. "I'll be fine, Mom." On her own. As always. "Thanks for everything."

"Because I could stay a couple more days if you…"

If she needed her? Well, she didn't. Not anymore. They'd successfully managed to check out of the hospital, evade the media and avoid rush-hour traffic. Now all Kenzie needed was a cup of something hot and some peace and quiet.

"You're going to miss your flight. Again," she said.

"You're sure?"

Kenzie nodded.

"Okay, then. I guess I'll head out." Her mother leaned close and grabbed Kenzie in an awkward hug.

Kenzie patted her back. "Have a good trip, Mom."

"All right." She pulled away and straightened her blouse. "Come see me sometime, you hear?"

Kenzie heard, but didn't make any promises as she followed her mother to the door and watched her pull away in a rental car before disappearing around a corner.

Finally. A few hours all to herself to finish out her spring break. But, stepping back inside, her home didn't give her the sense of peace she longed for. It just felt…abandoned.

Three visits were too many. Cole needed to fade into the background and let Kenzie forget about the worst day of her life. But the thought of roses forced him down the hospital corridor, to the room at the end. She'd had a bouquet of them—he had finally remembered setting his card beside the vase on his first visit. But how many roses made up the bouquet?

If it was an even half dozen, he'd wish her a wonderful life and bid her farewell. If there was just one more…

Kenzie's door was partially open. Cole knocked and gently pushed.

The bed was empty. The end table cleared off. Cole leaned against the door and stared into the shadowy space.

Now what?

A nurse tapped him on the arm. "You're the one that found MacKenzie Jacobs, right?"

Cole blinked and nodded. How did she know? He'd managed to avoid the media so far.

"How romantic," the nurse sighed. "Her mom took her home this morning, but she left this for you in case you came back." She held out one envelope, then pulled a smaller one out of her pocket. "And we found this after she left. It fell under the end table. Mind getting it to her when you see her again?" She fluttered her eyelashes at him, then smirked and walked away.

Cole opened the first envelope before he reached the bottom floor. A thank-you card with her phone number on it. Probably only so she could ask again how she could thank him.

He dialed the number as he slid the second envelope into the pocket of his jacket. Outside of the hospital, Cole paced the sidewalk as he waited for Kenzie to pick up the phone. His shoulders tensed a little more with each ring.

She was fine. Resting in her own house. Perfectly safe.

But he kept picturing the terrified girl on the cover of *Obsession* and remembering how many details the author had gotten right. And that the story hadn't ended there. But that was Monique. Not Kenzie.

He could remind himself of that all day, but it wouldn't calm his restlessness. He had to make sure she was okay.

"Hello?"

"Hi, Kenzie. It's Cole. They told me you'd checked out of the hospital. I wanted to make sure you got settled in okay..." And that she was still alive. And maybe see if she'd like to go out...

Right. With him—the detective's number-one suspect, although Parker had seemingly left him alone after his last interview. Maybe he'd decided to believe the polygraph results. More likely he was waiting for the warrant to come through to tap his phone line.

"Cole." Her voice was soft and sweet. "Yes, they let me go a few hours ago. It's so nice to be home."

His jaw tightened. Undoubtedly, she felt like she could put the whole thing behind her now. But it wasn't going to happen. He just knew.

So much for a relaxing, soul-searching vacation before starting another project. The paranoia just wouldn't let up. Not until he knew about the roses.

"I have something to ask you." He tried to form the question. Nothing. He closed his eyes, took a breath, pictured fear creeping back into those peaceful blue eyes. "I was wanting to talk, if you have time later." Coward. "Could I treat you to dinner? As a welcome-home present?" He squeezed the bridge of his nose as a different type of tension hit him. Who was the last woman he'd asked on a date?

Allison.

This was a huge mistake.

"That would be nice," she finally said. "Especially if you let me pay the bill."

"We'll haggle over that later. Just tell me where and when to pick you up."

Cole jotted down the directions to her house, then hung up and wandered to his rental car. What had he just done? They'd eat a relaxing meal before he predicted her dire future. What a great date he'd be. He should have just told her over the phone. Let her decide then if she still wanted to meet a nut-job like him. Instead, he'd have to actually see the expression on her face—first the one where he ripped away her sense of security, then the one where she called for a straitjacket.

Back at John's apartment, he checked the time. Another two hours before he needed to pick her up. Now that he'd made a fool of himself, there was something else he could be doing—something he *should* be doing. Reading the rest of *Obsession*, taking notes and finding out if anything else in the book had taken place. Like the flowers. That was as far as he'd gotten. Every time he picked up the book to read more, dread filled him. Like he was seeing into the future, and it was going to end badly.

Just do it, already.

He picked up the Warren Flint book and found his place, setting a notebook beside him. He found the notes he'd already taken. The dialogue that closely matched what he remembered from the bus, the black van, the roses and threatening card. Reading further, he scribbled "weird phone calls."

Creepy, but not so bad. Maybe Monique/Kenzie wouldn't go

through much after all. And if the cops kept an eye on her phone, maybe they could find out where the weird calls were from.

And all her other calls…

Cole's pencil drifted across the page. Parker would know he had called her. Would he find that suspicious? Probably. Cole couldn't blame him. He still wondered if he had somehow set the string of events into motion ~~ by bringing that stupid book on board.

Cole held open the heavy wooden door of the restaurant. Kenzie tugged her sweater closer as the air-conditioning hit her. Now that she was here, she wondered if she was making a mistake. She was out of her comfort zone, going out with a man she hardly knew. Unexpectedly, the tight quarters and unfamiliar atmosphere scared her, and she quickly searched the restaurant for a sinister face. Not that she knew what her abductors looked like, but maybe she'd be able to sense their presence.

Nothing.

Cole touched her shoulder for a brief, comforting moment, and Kenzie forced herself to walk normally, eyes straight ahead instead of glaring from right to left in paranoia. The hostess led them to a corner booth, and Cole slid into the seat across from Kenzie.

The soft-blue walls relaxed her while the dark wood tones of the furniture added a touch of class. Mismatched white china propped on shelves made for an unusual border a foot below the ceiling. Frames the same shade as the furniture encased sepia-toned photographs of families cooking together, and each table had an antique-looking white pitcher or crock holding blue flowers.

Her breathing came easier. Especially when he smiled and spoke her name.

"Have you eaten here before?"

"No," she said. "But I've been wanting to try it."

"Good choice." He nodded toward the corner, where a musician played a melancholy tune on an acoustic guitar.

"Thanks." She perused the menu for a moment, then leaned her head back and closed her eyes. She felt safe here. She even saw the comforting glow of the pendant lamp through her eyelids. She was still alive and almost happy.

A miracle.

And she owed at least part of that miracle to the man with the shaggy hair and soul-soothing voice.

"Tired?" he asked quietly.

"Not really. Mostly…content."

Opening her eyes, she studied him, remembered the way he'd held her when she was half-dead and scared out of her mind in the darkness of the boathouse. Looking at him, remembering the strength in his arms, the confidence in his gaze, the care in his voice…she could almost believe everything was going to be all right.

Cole watched Kenzie as she picked up the menu again. He was going to have to tell her sooner or later. He grimaced, imagining how the conversation could go. *So, Kenzie. I have a theory that someone is going to use a thriller as a blueprint of how to make the next few months of your life a living hell. Oh, and you're looking beautiful, by the way.*

She was, actually, with her thick brown mane shiny in the soft lamplight. He wanted to sketch her, just like this. Cole forced a smile as she slowly blinked at him as though just waking up, her dark lashes brushing her cheeks before her smoky-blue eyes met his. She seemed so different from the traumatized woman he'd carried out of the boathouse. Could he really plunge her back into that terror? It was just a crazy theory, after all. A weird sense of déjà vu...

The waitress arrived and took their order, then Kenzie leaned forward in her seat.

"So, tell me, Mr. Knight in Shining Armor." She winked. "What are you doing in Atlanta?"

Ah, there was a thought. Tell her about his own pathetic life so she didn't feel so bad about her own. "I'm visiting my cousin—you met John—and just doing some sight-seeing before I start another engineering project." One side of his mouth twisted up. Whether it came off as a half smile or a grimace, he wasn't sure.

"And how do you like Atlanta so far?"

Cole raised his eyebrows. "Well, it's been quite the ride, and I haven't even made it to Six Flags yet."

Kenzie ducked her head, but he caught the giggle, and it did more to warm him than the coffee the waitress had just delivered. It was good to see her like this, in everyday life, out of crisis mode.

And then he remembered the main reason he'd set up this little chat.

That could wait. First they'd have a pleasant dinner. Safe conversation—food, music, weather. It wouldn't be right to ruin her appetite with hypothetical threats. Right now maybe keeping a smile on her face was the most important thing he could do.

Kenzie groaned and pushed her pie plate toward Cole. His hair fell over one eye, giving him a slightly rakish look. But the man seated across from her—leaning his elbows on the table and glancing up to give her a rueful half smile—wasn't dangerous.

Or was he? Her heart already experienced free-fall sensations, and her breathing sometimes grew difficult as she looked into his eyes and drowned in their depths.

Very dangerous, indeed.

The waitress dropped off the check. Kenzie started to reach for it, but Cole's hand caught hers and held it gently. Crinkles appeared at the corners of his eyes as he smiled at her.

"I've got it covered."

"But I owe you…" Everything. She owed him absolutely everything. "Let me at least try to thank you in this small way. I'll be trying for the rest of my life."

His eyes changed, and he blinked. What had she said? Had she offended him in some way? He didn't let go of her, and his calloused fingers sent warm sparks up her arm.

"What is it?"

When he still didn't answer, she shifted her gaze to the door, then swept it around the nearly deserted restaurant. Nothing seemed threatening, so what…?

He traced her rope burns with his finger, his touch exquisite in its gentleness. So was his expression as he lifted his face.

"Kenzie, you don't owe me anything. What I did…I did it because God had His thumb in my back. I couldn't *not* do it, for my own sake." His jaw clenched, and he squeezed her hand lightly before letting go. "I'm no hero, Kenzie. Not even close. I'm just glad you're okay."

Blinking rapidly, Kenzie folded her hands in her lap. She searched for a change of subject—anything to keep tears from falling. "So how did you find me?" she blurted out.

Cole met her eyes, and his expression seemed to close. "It's a long, crazy story. You sure you're up for it?"

Probably not. But she wanted to hear it anyway. "Yes." That is, if she could make herself pay attention to his words instead of gawking at his handsome features. His five o'clock shadow did nothing to detract from his appearance. Did he have *any* flaws?

If he did, she didn't want to know about them. She'd rather look back on this evening, this moment, this memory, and feel like somewhere in the crazy world, there was a man who was, well, perfect.

Was this a mistake? It had felt like he was doing the heroic thing. But then, it had felt that way with Allison at first. And that had been wrong, all wrong. So what was he doing here?

Too late to back out now. Cole took another sip of his coffee, a steadying breath, and then dove in. "It all started with this book."

As he continued, Kenzie's dreamy expression rapidly faded, leaving only a ghost of color in its wake.

He finished, staring down at the table, unable to meet her eyes. "You have no idea how much I wish I had a different story to tell you, but that's what happened."

She was so silent he finally looked up to make sure she was still there. In a voice just above a whisper, she said, "Well...I'm just glad it's over."

"Kenzie..." If he didn't say it now, he never would. "That's just it. I don't think it's over."

"Don't say that, Cole."

"But here's the thing—"

"No. Don't do this to me." Panic made her words tumble over each other. "It's done. They're on the run, but they'll be caught soon. And my life *will be normal* once again."

"You have no idea how much I hope you're right. Just answer a couple questions for me and we'll probably have our answer, okay?"

"I *am* right." Her protest sounded weak.

"Okay. Let's find out. We know the whole hostage scenario

matches up, but maybe that was a fluke." Right. "Have you noticed anyone following you? Have you gotten any odd phone calls?"

"Cole, you're creeping me out."

"I know." He tightened his grip on the coffee mug to keep himself from reaching for her hand. "I'm sorry. I just want to make sure. I think this is really important."

"No. Okay? Just leave it alone. It's over and done with. I just want them caught and then I'm going to forget about the whole thing. *Every*thing. Even—"

Kenzie broke off, but Cole understood and flinched. *Even you.* Kenzie had made herself perfectly clear. Worse, he didn't blame her. It hurt more than he'd thought it would, tearing a hole in his heart.

She had tight control of herself when she spoke again. "What book is this?"

"*Obsession* by Warren Flint." He toyed with his cup, wondering if he should just get up and walk away.

She beat him to it.

Hot tears coursed down Kenzie's face as she shoved her way outside. As if she hadn't cried enough. But this time it was different; this time the tears were liquid frustration. She'd liked him. Really, *really* liked him. So why did he have to go and—

She stopped walking, then wiped at her eyes. Exactly how did she plan on getting home? The bus? The restaurant door opened again, but she stepped off the sidewalk without looking back.

The guy was nuts. His theory—totally off the wall. No wonder the detective had asked her about him.

The tension came back in waves, growing stronger with each step. Kenzie shifted her gaze to just past Cole's car, where the glow cast by the parking lot lights faded into black. Had something moved?

No. Just her imagination. She had to get a grip—

Her cell phone rang. In a rush of fury, she scooped it from her purse. "Leave me alone, Cole."

Silence.

"Cole?"

Nothing but the quiet ticking of a clock.

Cole slid some folded bills under the check and jerked to his feet. Kenzie didn't believe him. Well, that was her prerogative. He'd done what he could. Now he would drive her home and wash his hands of the whole thing.

He strode to the door, wondering if she'd even be on the other side. She was, standing under a floodlight in the middle of the parking lot, looking lost.

He waited until he was closer, then called out, "Kenzie, come on. Let me take you home."

He slowed his approach as she whirled to face him. "Why? So you can tell me more horrors that are in my future?"

"I'm sorry, Kenzie. I just want you to be—"

"Safe? I thought I was. And now I'm more afraid than before." She turned away as tears spilled down her cheeks.

"Kenzie, I'm sorry." For everything. For scaring her, for all that she'd been through, for…for not being able to wrap her in his arms and make everything okay. "Just let me take you home. I won't say another word."

Her eyes bored into him, then she gave a slight nod and led the way to his car.

Heavy silence filled the interior as he drove. Cole willed her to say something, anything. But she didn't, and he kept his promise. Not a word. He'd done what he could.

Then why didn't it feel like enough?

He parked in her driveway and walked her to the door, where he waited as she slid her key into the lock.

"I need to go," she finally said, her back to him as she stepped inside. "Thank you for the roses."

Shock jolted him forward. "Kenzie, I didn't—"

Too late. She slammed the door, and the dead bolt slid into place.

TEN

The pastor may have touched heaven in his sermon, but all Kenzie felt was the vibrating of her cell phone. Unknown number. Maybe it was the police department. Maybe it was Cole Leighton.

Maybe it was just the anonymous ticking of a clock.

Whatever it was, whoever it may be, Kenzie couldn't look away from it. The service ended, and the phone buzzed again.

"Miss Jacobs." Her principal stopped beside her seat. "MacKenzie. I wanted to catch you before you left."

Heat stained her cheeks as she lowered the phone, keeping it in a tight, clammy hold. "Dr. Anderson. Thanks so much for the carnations."

"It was the least we could do. I hear you're planning on teaching tomorrow?" His brown eyes studied her, the wrinkle in his forehead hinting at his concern.

"Yes. I'm fine." Kenzie ran her free hand over her hair, hoping the scratches on her face had faded. "Just a little tired and bruised."

The phone buzzed again, just once. A message.

Don't look.

She forced herself to smile at her boss. To say whatever she needed to say to convince him she was all right. She needed to work, needed to see her kids, hear their laughter. Focus on things that were good before the bad overwhelmed her.

Dr. Anderson finally walked away, and Kenzie pressed the button to call her voice mail and slowly settled the phone against her ear. No familiar voice greeted her. No telemarketer told her how much she needed help with her mortgage. Only silence, then the same ominous ticking.

Should she call Cole? Ask him for his definition of "odd" phone calls? Kenzie bit her lip, closed her eyes as she wavered...

Then punched the off button and threw the cell in her bag.

Routine was good. Getting back into teaching mode, seeing the students she'd missed even more than she'd realized, having a task to complete—it helped Kenzie feel normal. Safe.

So, even though she was exhausted, Kenzie stayed true to her Monday schedule and found a ride to the gym. Half an hour of circuit training, and then home.

There, Kenzie dragged herself to the bedroom, flipping on all the lights as she passed through the house. She changed into jeans and returned to the living room. The light on the answering machine blinked. Three messages. One from Detective Parker—no new leads. Had she remembered anything else, and was she doing okay? In other words, had anything suspicious happened? Not unless you counted... No. Cole was a nut case. The weird calls were just a coincidence.

The next message was the auto shop asking her to call at her earliest convenience. Kenzie sighed—probably meant the fix was an expensive one and they wanted her go-ahead. Well, that could wait until tomorrow. She'd already arranged for a ride to work.

The final message was that same annoying ticktock. Then the dial tone.

It's just a wrong number, she told herself.

So why did her breathing come in ragged gasps?

Kenzie stalked to the kitchen and yanked open the refrigerator door. Something nice, warm and homemade sounded like the perfect supper. She'd make some soup, do a little whittling and take another shower to wash off the stress of the day.

She pulled vegetables out of the refrigerator and started chopping, calling her mother to check in and fill the silence. Even though their conversation was stilted, Kenzie felt herself slowly calm down.

Until she turned to the sink, faced the window and felt eyes watching…waiting.

Whose idea had it been to come to Atlanta? Sure, Cole needed space to think and heal, if healing was a possibility for someone so broken. But why here? Where his cousin stared with eyes that saw too much and tried to make him back into the man he used to be…

"The small groups meeting is tomorrow night," John said. "It's just going to be some of the teen guys and me. No big deal."

Cole forced down a bite of egg roll. "Not going to happen."

"But Cole, you could be a really great influence on them—"

"I'm a burned out civil engineer, John. How exactly is that going to help anybody?" Cole scooped up some lo mein, but it suddenly tasted like the box it came in. Who was he to try to teach kids anything? He was just a guy who made a mess of things.

John cocked his head and narrowed his eyes. "What's going on with you, Cole?"

Cole kept his focus on the food. He was in no mood to be psychoanalyzed.

Letting the moment pass, John said, "They'll see you as a hero. They know about how you rescued the girl from the bus."

Kenzie. He'd spent all weekend trying not to think about her. The worry hit him once again in full force. Thanks a lot, John.

"So come talk to the kids. It'll do them good. And you, too."

"No." Cole finally met his cousin's eyes. Time for a little honesty. "God and I aren't on the best of terms."

He pushed away from the table, accidentally knocking over his water glass. Liquid streamed off the wood surface onto a chair, the jacket thrown across the seat…and the envelope sticking out of the jacket pocket. The envelope he'd forgotten to deliver to Kenzie.

He snatched it up as John threw a dish towel over the spill. One side of the envelope flopped downward from the weight of the water. Blotting it with a napkin didn't help much. Ruined. He couldn't give—no…*send* it to her like that.

Cole carefully peeled back the soggy paper to expose the note within.

Till we meet again.

Clutching the book in clammy fingers, Cole punched Kenzie's doorbell. His nerves jangled as he listened for her approach. He wanted to see her, yet dreaded the moment when she would open the door…if she actually did. He paced back and forth on the small porch. Two steps, turn, two steps more.

"What are you doing here?" Kenzie asked sharply.

Cole whirled to face her. "Kenzie, I know you don't want

to talk to me." How long did he have before she slammed the door in his face? Again? "But please hear me out, just this once. I promise not to bother you anymore."

She huffed a breath and folded her arms, drawing his attention to what she held in her hands. A knife, blade winking in the porch light. Either she'd taken him seriously after all, or she hated him more than he'd figured. He backed down a step.

"As much as I'd like to, I'm not going to stab you," Kenzie said, rolling her eyes.

Maybe not, but she was good at inserting verbal blades between his ribs.

"I just want to help, Kenzie. That's it."

Actually it wasn't. He'd also like to see her smile again, make her laugh, watch the cares melt off her face, take her out to dinner to try to make up for the last one.

But none of that was going to happen, and that was probably for the best.

"Then come in and get it over with." Her gaze darted over his shoulder, and then she stepped aside.

Taking a deep breath, Cole forced himself to walk with confidence. He had nothing to be ashamed of. Well, not here, at least. Kenzie motioned him to an overstuffed armchair, where he obediently sat. She settled onto the microfiber sofa, kitty-corner from him. The knife still in her hands, she picked up a whetstone and set to work.

The television played in the background, but for a moment all he could do was stare as she scraped blade against stone. Now who was the creepy one?

"Look, I like to whittle, okay?" Kenzie finally said. She pulled a block of wood from a basket on the floor. "See? I'm not preparing to flay you alive, so just spit out whatever you came to tell me."

Cole blinked, then chuckled and leaned back slightly. "You whittle?"

"Yeah. I don't like to just sit. Have to do something with my hands, so…" She motioned to the chess set beside him.

Cole picked up a hand-carved queen, studying the exquisite detail. "Wow." The set was nearly complete, only lacking a couple of pawns. "These are great, but can't you just…knit, or something?"

Kenzie bit her lip. From annoyance, or was she forcing back a laugh? "Stop changing the subject."

"Fine." He extended Warren Flint's novel, sliding it across the wooden trunk that served as a coffee table. "I wanted to bring this over. Have you read it?"

Kenzie inspected the block of wood in her hands and shook her head.

"Well, I don't want you to take my word for it—I want you to read it yourself and see how close the bus scene matched. And I want you to see what else happens in the book, see if any of it has happened to you so you can tell me…" Cole sighed. Right. Like she would put him on speed dial or something. "Or Detective Parker. Then maybe the police can figure out how to catch them, how to make it stop."

"Make what stop, Cole?" Her voice was calm, but she still wouldn't favor him with a look. Probably better that way. Otherwise, she might turn him to stone with her glare.

She carefully examined the wood, probably deciding where to make the first cut, how to find the shape of the pawn in the heart of the balsa. Humoring him but not really listening, not realizing *she* was the pawn. Nothing he could say would convince her of that. She'd have to see it with her own eyes. Feel herself being played.

"Just read it, Kenzie," he said softly. "Please. If you want to talk when you're done, I stuck my number in the book. And if not, I won't come around anymore."

Head bowed, she remained seated as he walked toward the door, opened it and twisted the lock before closing it behind him. *Use your dead bolt, Kenzie.* But he didn't say it out loud. His work here was done.

Kenzie didn't realize she was crying until she noticed wet splotches on the wood. Maybe instead of whittling, she should crawl under the covers and never come out.

Wimp.

Well, whatever she did, she was *not* going to read that book.

The theme song for a talk show caught her attention. She raised her eyes to the screen and blinked hard as a man wearing an affable smile waved from his leather chair on the set.

New York Times best-selling author Warren Flint. And, if the book the host, Barry Bowman, held in his hands was any indication, they were talking about *Obsession.*

Apparently she hadn't raised her quota of goose bumps for the day.

She exchanged the knife for the remote and cranked the volume as the cheering died down.

"So, Warren, a few more questions about *Obsession* before we move on to your newest thriller, coming out tomorrow." Bowman smiled, his perfectly straight and gleaming teeth appearing artificial.

Tuning him out, Kenzie shifted her gaze to the book on the coffee table. Right side up, the title laughed up at her in bold red print. She cringed at the darkness of it, the terrified face on the cover—her face—that seemed to morph into a genuine scream.

She shoved it off the trunk and reached again for the knife.

"Tell us, Warren, where did you get the inspiration for *Obsession*? Especially for Monique."

"It was at a book signing in Atlanta." Flint looked off set, seemingly replaying the scene in his mind. "I met a fascinating young woman—a teacher at a Christian school. Gentle and soft-spoken, but with something in her eyes…"

Kenzie raised an eyebrow and made the first cut into the balsa wood.

"Something that said she was stronger than she realized. And right there, Monique began to take shape. A beautiful woman pitted against insurmountable odds, yet finding the inner strength to fight back."

Stronger than she realized? Then why was she here, her trembling fingers gripping Mikey's old pocketknife, hiding scared from the world? The woman the author thought he'd seen didn't exist.

Of course, neither did Monique.

"In fact, this is my favorite cover for all my books, because…" Flint tapped the face of the woman on the glossy book-jacket. "This is her. Monique *and* the real-life version."

Why was she watching this? Oh, to keep from hiding under the covers. Like this was helping. Kenzie concentrated on the wood, the form she wanted to find within it.

Never again would she model for a book cover. Never. And if she wasn't already on shaky spiritual ground, she'd curse the day she met Warren Flint. If she remembered right, she'd given the autographed book to Coach Bryan for his birthday. A hit that sparked a short crush that ended in a little more heartbreak for her. Yeah, she could have done without the whole Warren Flint episode of her life.

"Now the ending is a bit…ambiguous," Bowman said. "Some people think Monique lived, some aren't so sure."

Kenzie's hands stilled as she watched the screen once again.

"Do you have any hints as to which camp we should be in? Or was it a setup for a sequel?"

Flint smiled and smiled until quiet laughter came from the audience. "I wasn't going to answer that, but I think I will, after all. It'll be the first time."

"An exclusive!" Bowman's teeth gleamed in the studio lights.

Kenzie leaned forward, barely breathing, feeling as her life depended on the author's answer.

Flint nodded, then paused as if mulling it over. "I write as my characters speak to me. When they stop, the story is over. So—"

"Monique stopped talking to you." Bowman's eyes grew round. "Does that mean she's dead?"

Kenzie's hand slipped, and the knife sliced into her palm. Biting her lip, she clenched a hand around the wound and listened for his answer. Not that she thought Cole was right, but still. If she was the author's inspiration for Monique, well, she would prefer to know the heroine lived on in Flint's mind. Seemed...*safer* that way.

And maybe if she knew Monique lasted to the end, she could laugh off Cole's warnings, switch to an unlisted number and get on with her life.

"No, not necessarily," Flint said. "It just means this story was over. Maybe she's dead. Maybe she'll talk to me again and make a comeback. Maybe she's alive but doesn't have anything else to say."

"So it's up to the reader to decide," Bowman said.

"Absolutely." Flint turned to the audience. "What did Monique say to *you?*"

Kenzie jabbed the power button. Gripping her bleeding hand, she stared at the blank screen.

ELEVEN

Cole blew out a breath and stared through the window of the apartment. The police had staked it out for a while. Oh, they'd stayed out of his way. They were just staying close enough to catch him in a wrong move.

Well, that wrong move had happened the moment he'd first seen MacKenzie Jacobs. But they couldn't bring him in for that.

He'd given her two days—plenty of time to at least start reading the book—but she hadn't called. Probably hadn't even cracked the cover. He needed to move on, forget about her, go ahead and leave town. But, God help him, he was deathly afraid she was going to get killed on his watch.

She's not yours to lose.

No. She wasn't. He had to let go and trust God to take care of her. Why couldn't he do that? Because he had to be the hero, and heroes didn't let someone else do the work. How pathetic was he? He'd like to be normal for once. Get rid of his knight-in-shining-armor complex. Go eat with the guys and check out the waitress just because she had a pretty smile, not because her eyes seem haunted.

Cole shoved the last of his clothes into his suitcase and threw his sketchbook on top with more force than necessary.

Yeah, he had issues. One of these days he'd conquer them. Maybe. He'd start by leaving town and never seeing Kenzie Jacobs again.

As much as he'd like to.

Closing his eyes, he pictured her: shiny, dark hair; sad eyes the color of blueberries, a beautiful but too-rare smile. He wanted to help her, to protect her. To calm her fears and be the hero in her life. Instead, he'd been the cause of more fear.

It had to stop. Right now.

Kenzie stood under the stream of water, waiting for the heat to warm her chilled skin. Hopefully the warmth would make its way to the inside, coursing through her bloodstream, curling around her heart.

But her teeth continued to chatter as she poured shower gel onto a pouf, massaged shampoo into her scalp and scrubbed exfoliating cleansers into her face. If only she could scrub off the past week as easily. Just take off the top layer. Gone. Something fresh and new ready to take its place.

Still cold, Kenzie stepped out of the shower and dressed, then twisted her damp hair into a knot. The dripping ends escaped as she clipped the rest in place, but the water slipping inside her collar wasn't the cause of the icy fingers tickling her spine.

She heard talking…music…something that shouldn't be there.

"I don't think it's over." She remembered Cole Leighton's grave voice, imagined the reluctant concern in his eyes, the fear in the tightening of his lips. No. It *was* over—had to be. The radio must have clicked on. Her alarm messed up somehow. Her landlord let himself in to check on the broken stove. Something…

But she picked up her heavy-duty curling iron just in case. She turned the knob, held her weapon ready, stepped back. The door creaked open.

No attack. No intruder.

And no lights. None at all, except for a blue glow coming from the living room, from the television that she hadn't turned on since Monday. Someone was in her house.

Panic hit—doubling her over, leaving her fighting for air. *It's not over.* Would it ever be?

She had to get control. Get out. Get away. But the closest exit was the front door—through the living room, past the flickering television. She could hear the music more clearly now. Old horror-flick stuff. Peering into the room, she searched the blue shadows. Nothing. Just the television. Holding the curling iron like a small club, Kenzie stepped forward. No movement.

Another step.

Violins screeched. A voice screamed over and over again, drawing her gaze to the screen. Kenzie stopped in front of the television. Froze.

Then she screamed, too.

"Griggs. I found something."

Kenzie followed Officer Griggs with her eyes as he strode over to his partner, but the policeman's wide back blocked her view. Fine. She didn't really want to see what they held in their hands. Evidence of an intruder. Proof that a stalker existed.

Sinking back into the couch cushions, she closed her eyes and tried to keep her mind blank. It didn't work.

"Miss Jacobs?"

She opened her eyes to find Officer Griggs staring at her with squinty eyes.

"Could you describe again what happened?"

"Again?" These guys must have the attention span of her first-graders.

"Please."

Kenzie gave a slight shake of her head, hoped he didn't see it. She took a breath, held it in and somehow found the strength to go through it once more. When she got to the part where she had stood in front of the television, the tremors started again. She just wanted to leave the house. Skip town. Her teacher's aide would be glad to take her place.

"And then? What was on the screen?"

She didn't understand. It was right there, on Pause. They could watch it themselves. "The same scene played over and over—looping somehow." She squeezed her eyes shut. "There was the sound of running water. A woman taking a shower. The shadow of someone approaching, holding a…knife. The curtain opened, and—" Kenzie swallowed hard. In her mind, the woman was *her*. The knife stabbed *her* flesh. The blood running down the drain, *hers*. Obviously the stalker's intention: *This is what I could have done to you.* "He killed her. Then it played all over again." And again and again as she stood there, screaming in the dark until the cops showed up in response to her neighbor's phone call.

"Hitchcock's infamous shower scene," the other policeman said.

"I guess." Kenzie looked up at them. "I never saw it. I don't enjoy that kind of thing." Not suspense, mysteries, not even roller coasters.

"Someone made that scene even more infamous," Officer Griggs said.

His partner handed him a book, and Kenzie's insides turned to dust. No. This was some insane nightmare. She'd wake up soon, and then she'd kick Cole all the way back to wherever he came from for making her so paranoid.

"Harrison found this on your nightstand. Don't like Hitchcock, but you'll read a Warren Flint thriller to help you sleep, huh?"

The nightstand? She'd left it by the door, ready to go to the trash or the thrift store or to throw at Cole's head if he showed up again.

Cole. Oh, God, don't let him be right.

"How do you explain this, Miss Jacobs?" He opened the book and shoved it in her face, his blunt finger marking the beginning of a paragraph.

> *Rivulets of water streamed from her hair. Down her neck, onto her back, occasionally dripping from her cheeks. Monique's chills came from somewhere else, from a fear deep inside. She heard running water. It roared in her ears, louder than the music and the screams. Rushing water mixed with blood as the actress was stabbed to death.*

"Huh," Griggs said. "You even look like her."

Kenzie slammed the book shut. She couldn't read anymore. Of course, she didn't have to, did she? Because it was all being acted out for her in real time.

Her life. Monique's. The same.

Cole picked up his cell phone and answered without looking away from traffic. He said a gruff hello and felt his pulse pound in his throat as he heard soft crying on the other end. Kenzie.

"What's wrong?"

She gave a shuddering gasp. "Someone's been in my house."

"What?" He swung into the turning lane without clicking on the blinker. "Where are you?"

"Still home. The police are about to leave. But…can you come?"

His breath hitched at the break in her voice. "I'm on my way."

"I—I think you might be right."

Jabbing his fingers through his hair, he pressed the gas pedal harder. "What happened, Kenzie?"

Voices sounded in the background. "I have to go," Kenzie said into the phone. "Just get here. Please."

He'd planned on driving by anyway, just to make sure one more time that she was okay before he left town.

"Three minutes." Cole took a corner faster than he should have; the back right tire went over the curb but didn't slow him.

After the cops left, Kenzie hugged her knees to her chest and counted to sixty. Two minutes until Cole would stand at her door. Two minutes until she could talk to someone who believed her. She could ask if he was truly serious about his theory—although she figured she knew the answer to that already—ask how he'd guessed that someone had decided to use her to act out Warren Flint's novel, find out why he even cared whether she listened to him or not.

A minute and a half.

She needed him to tell her who was doing this and why. And how they could be stopped. But, of course, he wouldn't know. It was only a theory.

She began to shake again.

What if Cole was serious about his theory because…he was in on it? Because he was the one reading the book and masterminding the whole thing? He'd probably been the one she felt watching her earlier, probably waited across the street even now, counting down the seconds himself until he could waltz in as rescuer. Again. Maybe he'd whisk her away to somewhere "safe" and then launch phase two of whatever horrors awaited her in the pages of Flint's book. How else could he get here in five minutes? This was Atlanta.

Then why would he warn her? Why would he bring her home after her abduction? Why would he give her the book?

To show her what would happen next. To enhance the cat-and-mouse games. To paralyze her with fear.

Well, he wouldn't have to make her read a thriller to do that—he could just turn out the lights.

But not Cole. He was crazy, yes. But he was a good guy. Right?

The doorbell rang.

TWELVE

Cole stood back, keeping an eye on the street as he waited for Kenzie to answer the door. He racked his brain, trying to call up the list he'd made while reading *Obsession*. The only thing he could remember happening in Monique's house was...the *Psycho* scene. Which still gave him the creeps.

He faced the door just as it creaked open. Kenzie stood there, pale and trembling, her eyes searching his as she blocked the entrance.

"Tell me you didn't do this, Cole."

Cole took a small step back. "What's going on, Kenzie?"

"Why don't you tell me?" It wasn't an accusation...yet.

"I'm here to help, Kenzie. I promise. Whatever just happened, I'm not the bad guy." It stung that she could think that. But it must be less scary to blame someone she could see than to face an unknown threat.

She stood there, leaning against the door frame in indecision. His hand raised of its own accord—he wanted to push back her damp hair, kiss away the tears that hovered near the surface.

She flinched, and he jerked his hand back. What was he thinking?

"Tell me what happened, Kenzie. I swear I didn't do it.

Why don't you let me in, then tell me what's going on and we'll figure out a plan, okay?"

She stared at him, searching his face, then stepped aside and held open the door. He cautiously walked through, half expecting a blow to the back of his skull. When it didn't come, he turned to find her leaning her forehead against the closed door.

Cole reached out again but caught himself before he made contact. His entire being ached to hold her, to protect her, to fix everything. But the last time he'd tried that, with another woman, in another place, he'd made things infinitely worse. So he remained still, giving her space. *God, don't let me mess up again.*

When would it end? Or maybe the better question was how. Who was doing this to her?

Kenzie lifted her face from her hands to meet Cole's scrutiny. He sat on the floor, his legs bent and his arms draped around his knees as he leaned against a bookshelf. Against her better judgment, she trusted the man. He'd saved her life. He'd soothed her. He came when she called, not afraid to face her fears. And not dismissing them—that might be the most important thing.

"So now what?" She hated how her voice quavered.

"First of all, are you sure you're okay?"

Occasional tremors still shook her, but she was alive and safe. For the moment. "Yes."

"Good." His gaze flitted around the room then back to her. "Let's get out of here."

"Okay." Relief made her weak, and Kenzie choked back tears. She shouldn't be glad to flee her own home. "Should I bring anything?"

Cole paused. "The book. Stuff for a little trip. I don't think you should stay here tonight."

She sucked in a breath. "Where are we going?"

His eyes flickered. "Not sure." He looked like he wanted to say more, but he stared around the room once again and firmed his lips.

Logic battled against instinct, but the calm assurance in his sea-blue eyes won her over. "Give me five minutes."

"You got it."

Kenzie stepped into the hallway, but then her legs turned to lead. "Cole?" She'd barely been able to force out his name, but he appeared at her side a second later.

"What's wrong?"

"Can you… Would you mind staying with me while I pack?" Oh, she was so incredibly weak.

His hand touched her shoulder. "Anything you need."

Deep down, she knew he meant it. Her cheeks burned hot as she led him down the hallway, first to the closet to retrieve a duffel bag, then to her bedroom. Cole respectfully turned his back as she gathered her things.

"How many days should I pack for?"

Cole pivoted to face her, but shook his head. "We'll figure it out in the car." His eyes telegraphed something. A warning? About what?

His face tipped back as if he studied the ceiling, then he looked at her again.

It hit her like a wall of ice. The house could be bugged. Maybe he was even looking for cameras.

Kenzie threw clothes into the duffel. With Cole following, she raced to the bathroom and tossed in her toiletry bag, then barely paused in the living room to scoop up her brother's knife before barreling out the front door.

This was her home. Why did it suddenly feel like a house of horrors?

* * *

Cole loaded Kenzie's things into the trunk, then began to explain as soon as they pulled onto the road. "The book didn't spell everything out—it was all told from Monique's point of view, so this is guesswork. To set the stage for the *Psycho* thing, they had to know you were in the shower. Probably they'd gotten in there before and planted bugs or something. I didn't want to talk inside the house, just in case."

"I understand."

He didn't need to look at her to gauge her reaction. His skin already prickled for her. "Do you want to get out of town for a while? Stay with your parents?"

"It's only my mom, and no." Kenzie's forceful reply caught him off guard, but she kept talking before he could respond. "Spring break is over; school just started back up. I don't want to take any days off."

A good excuse, but Cole sensed it was just that—an excuse. "Fine. But we need to find somewhere else for you to stay."

"I could check into a hotel. Someone could look for bugs at the house. I'll add more locks. And then, just…" Her voice faded into silence.

Cole kept both hands on the steering wheel to stop himself from reaching for her.

"Cole, he could have killed me. Again."

His knuckles turned white as he clutched the wheel tighter. "But he didn't, okay? God kept you safe before, and He'll keep doing so. No one can send you to eternity before your time." He knew that for a fact; he'd tempted fate more than once.

When she remained silent, Cole gave her a sideways glance. Her face was stark white, framed by clumps of still damp hair, and her wide eyes stared blindly out the windshield.

"You're safe right now, Kenzie. We'll figure something out to keep you that way."

"Okay." Her flat tone conveyed resignation.

Come on, Kenzie. Fight. "Does Parker know about the intruder?"

"I don't know. I didn't call him. He wasn't with the police officers who came."

"He needs to know. But first, tell me the truth. Have you been getting odd phone calls—like with a clock ticking in the background?"

She paused. "Yes."

"And were there seven roses in that bouquet in your hospital room?"

Dead silence. Then, "You didn't send them."

"No, Kenzie."

No point in telling her about the card he'd never delivered. He slammed the steering wheel, then steadied himself, breathing hard. Traumatizing Kenzie wasn't enough. Now her home was violated…

"You need to tell Parker this. All of it."

"You figured it out. Why don't you tell him?"

Cole sucked in a breath. "I tried. He doesn't believe me." Or if he did, only because he suspected that Cole was the one doing the playacting.

"Fine. I'll tell him."

"I'll drop you off at the police station. Call me when you're done."

Kenzie crossed her legs, then uncrossed them, unable to get comfortable. She wished Cole had come inside with her. His presence alone would warm Parker's office. But he'd driven off with the phone to his ear.

Detective Parker opened the door and stepped inside, shuffling papers. His eyes were kind when they found hers. "Miss Jacobs, I'm glad you're feeling better, and I'm sorry this case hasn't been closed yet. I just want you to know we're working hard on it."

Kenzie nodded her thanks as the policeman settled his bulk into his desk chair.

"Why don't you go ahead and run me through everything that's happened since you were released from the hospital."

Closing her eyes, she tried to relax, then spelled it all out, this time including the phone calls and the roses and Cole's theory. Detective Parker kept silent, only interrupting when he needed her to clarify something. Then she stopped talking and opened her eyes. She didn't know what she'd hoped to see—a widening of his eyes that exclaimed, "I've solved it!" Or maybe a file shoved her way, asking her to confirm a suspect as the guy who had the honeyed voice with a Caribbean twist?

Instead, the detective rested his elbows on the desk and studied her.

Kenzie tried not to grimace. "Just say it. Whatever bad news you have…" She'd deal with it. Somehow.

"How well do you know Cole Leighton?"

The room suddenly seemed colder. Kenzie folded her arms across her chest and shifted in her seat. "Well, obviously, he saved my life. He's from Texas, in town on vacation. He's staying with his cousin, John Brennan." And he had unruly hair, vibrant eyes and the most kissable scruffy jaw—

Kenzie blushed and reined in her thoughts.

"You said in the hospital that you'd never met him before that day on the bus."

"Yes. That's right."

"You haven't recalled running into him before that?"

"No. Never."

The detective leaned back in his chair. "Has his behavior seemed odd at all to you?"

Kenzie frowned. "Odd, how?"

He didn't answer.

"Cole is a nice guy—really nice," she continued. "I mean, he went out of his way to help a stranger more than once. Is that considered odd?"

Detective Parker remained silent, probably hoping she'd spill some convicting bit of knowledge about the man who'd saved her life.

Despite the fact that she'd been suspicious of him, too, Kenzie felt her defenses rise, warding away the chill. "I don't know him well, but from what I've seen, he's a true gentleman. A good man. If that's odd, it shouldn't be."

The police officer raised his eyebrows and the silence grew heavier. "You could be right, Miss Jacobs. But it's only fair to warn you that Leighton is our top suspect at the moment."

"But that's crazy." Sudden anger flared. "There's no way—"

"Oh, I know he has a solid alibi—I was the one who interviewed him while your kidnappers transported you to that boathouse. But we think he could be involved. We just can't prove it."

Kenzie swallowed back a niggling doubt and spoke in a stern teacher voice. "You have the wrong man."

"Miss Jacobs—"

Kenzie's cell phone rang. Glad for an excuse to cut him off, she pulled it out of her handbag and checked the number. "Detective, I'm supposed to pick up my car from the auto shop. Would you mind…?"

He sighed and waved her on, but the tightening of his mouth suggested he saw through her excuse. "One of my officers will drive you. I'll give you a call later."

* * *

Cole entered the police station. Kenzie wasn't waiting for him. She hadn't called to tell him she was ready, either. Maybe Parker had her flipping through mug shots to see if she recognized anyone, or maybe he actually had a lineup.

Or maybe Parker had found out about his past, and Kenzie—

A pain shot through his chest—a sharp jab to his heart. Cole grimaced and rubbed a hand against his polo shirt, trying to wipe out the thought that Kenzie might know the truth about him. That she might distrust him. And yet, wasn't that what he deserved?

He was getting too close to her, and that couldn't happen.

Before he could connect with Kenzie, Cole found himself being ushered into an interview room. His gut clenched as Parker sat across from him, wearing a grim smile.

"I'm surprised to see you're still in town, Leighton. Still on vacation?"

"I'm still here." Cole ground his teeth and forced himself to maintain eye contact. Parker was only trying to set him on edge.

"I see. So why don't you run me through your version of what happened today?" In other words, did he have an alibi? At least this meant the authorities would take the incident seriously.

Parker took notes while Cole recounted his day, then he raised his head. Cole refused to shrink under the intense scrutiny.

"Since you're the one who suspected it first, I just wanted you to know the team I sent to Miss Jacobs's house did find a number of listening devices throughout the house."

Not cameras. At least Kenzie had maintained that much privacy.

"Interesting that you would have thought that…" the detective continued.

"It just made sense."

The air crackled, and Cole fought the urge to turn his head away.

"Do you know this woman?" Parker slid a photo across the table.

Even though he'd been half expecting it, Cole flinched when he saw Allison's face. "Yes. I knew her."

"And what was your relationship with her?"

Cole gritted his teeth.

"I understand." Parker sounded almost sympathetic. "We'll come back to that question."

Cole focused on the spot between Parker's eyes, intent on keeping a blank face. The guilt he felt would be misinterpreted. What he had done wrong wasn't anything an American court would try him for.

No, the consequences for his wrongdoing were eternal.

"So you knew Allison Watts, and you were living in Lubbock, Texas, three years ago when she had her *accident*, correct?"

"Yes, sir."

"What happened? Do you remember?"

"Yes." He dreamed about it—running beside the car and telling her to stop. Of standing in the middle of the road to flag her down. Nothing ever worked; nothing ever brought her back. "Her brakes gave out. She lost control and hit a tree."

Parker scribbled something. Maybe he'd seen Cole's left eyelid spasm. Or maybe he had X-ray vision and saw the shame coloring Cole's heart black.

"There was suspicion of sabotage, did you know that?"

Cole allowed a brief nod, his face as expressionless as

possible. He couldn't deny it. Parker had to have known he was the prime suspect. "It was ruled an accident."

"Yes." Parked shifted in his chair and rustled some papers. "I see that. I just thought it was interesting. A girl you were involved with in Texas winds up dead after an accident where there's suspicion of foul play. And you still showed up at the scene.

"Then, far from home, a girl you seem highly interested in has car trouble. Lo and behold, that very same day she nearly dies. You're on vacation in the area and happen to be at the scene. What a coincidence." Parker's eyes bored jagged holes through Cole's chest. "Oh, that's right. You don't believe in coincidences."

THIRTEEN

"Kenzie, it's good to see you." The owner of Dave's Auto Shop leaned across the counter. "You all right? I heard what happened."

Kenzie blushed. "I'm fine, thanks. The real question is, is my Honda okay?"

Dave frowned and tapped the bill he had waiting for her. "She's great. But there's something I need to talk to you about."

She tensed as he came around the counter and motioned her into the waiting room, away from listening ears. She wasn't that far behind in her bills, was she?

"Anybody been messing with your car recently?"

"I haven't been trying to change my oil, if that's what you're asking."

"It's not, because I would have known if you tried."

Kenzie gave a wry smile. "Dave, if I didn't know better, I'd say you just insulted my mechanical abilities."

"I was the one who worked on that poor Accord the first time you brought her in, remember?" He returned her smile briefly. "But I'm serious, Kenzie."

She shook her head. "No one's touched it. Why? What was wrong with it?"

He glanced at the bill, then handed it to her as he explained. "I had to do some troubleshooting to find out why there was no spark to your spark plugs. Kenzie, a rotor was missing, and the distributor cap was reinstalled to hide it."

Kenzie stared at him blankly, sure that was all supposed to mean something.

He looked her straight in the eye and sighed. "Someone sabotaged your car."

No. She stared at the mechanic, shaking her head. No, no, no. Was there anything they hadn't touched? Anywhere they hadn't been? How long had someone been watching her? Kenzie bit her trembling lower lip, trying to hold back the panic. She wouldn't scream, wouldn't cry. Not here.

"Dave, you mind if I…" She stared at the paper in her hand, but the figures were blurred.

"You just pay me when you can. And tell the police about this. I need my favorite customer to stay safe."

"Thanks, Dave," she whispered. "I'll get you a check by next week."

By the time she reached her car, her trembling legs could barely hold her up. She collapsed into the driver's seat, her feet crumpling the paper floor-mat with the Dave's Auto logo on it.

What else did the kidnappers have planned for her?

She should call Parker, but she'd rather talk to Cole. She tried his cell. No answer. Parker didn't answer, either, and she left a message, telling him what Dave had said.

Cole was probably with Parker—when he'd come to the station to pick her up, the detective had probably dragged Cole into one of those rooms to interrogate him.

Kenzie's hands left sweat marks on the steering wheel as she guided her car back toward the police station. Relief hit as soon as it came into sight and Kenzie saw Cole's car exiting the lot. She followed him, wanting to spill her news and take whatever advice he had to give. But when he pulled into a parking lot of a bookstore, she lost him. The spaces were filled to overflowing. She kept circling and felt the tremors return as the sky began to darken.

A spot finally opened up. She turned off the ignition and sat there, staring at the bookstore. So many people. Strangers. Potential enemies.

She double-checked the locks. Still no sign of Cole. Her heart squeezed, making it hard to breathe.

Someone sabotaged your car.

What if that someone was here? Buying out the store's supply of *Obsession*? Maybe they needed more copies on hand to give to recruits for their next stunt.

She needed to stop thinking, stop agonizing. Just go find Cole. She threw open the door and half jogged toward the building.

He should have just driven away, washing his hands of everything, running from false accusations.

God...

Cole couldn't find the courage to finish the prayer. He deserved the suspicious glances, the probing questions. But though he lived with his past every waking moment, he'd hoped that as far as everyone else was concerned, it had stayed buried in Lubbock after he'd moved. Was it fair—?

Life wasn't fair. Hadn't he taught that to Allison's husband?

A bitter taste filled Cole's mouth. No, life wasn't fair. And right now, someone else was passing the lesson on to Kenzie. Which was why he was at the bookstore. Again. It was time to find out if the creator of *Obsession* had become obsessed.

The line of fans was long, Cole's list of questions longer. As he waited with a new copy of the book firmly gripped in his hand, Cole studied the author—first in the promotional photo, then in person as he grew closer—searching for any hint of malevolence lurking under the man's polished demeanor.

"Good evening," Flint said, his face tired but friendly when Cole reached him. "Who would you like me to sign this to?" He stretched out a hand for Cole's book.

Cole plunked it onto the hard surface of the table. "Do you know a woman named MacKenzie Jacobs?" Anger shook his voice, and he gripped the underside of the table in an attempt to rid himself of it. Flint might not deserve suspicion any more than Cole had—but he doubted it.

The author's eyes flicked over the cover, then back to Cole. "We've met. What can I do for you?"

The line still snaked through the bookshelves. This was a bad time for confrontations, but it was now or never.

"You can tell me why you decided to act your story out on her."

Flint jerked his head back and stared from the cover to Cole and then to the people waiting behind him. "I don't know what you're talking about," he finally said.

Cole's stomach knotted. Any second now he'd probably be kicked out. "The bus, the hostage situation, the shower scene…that's all happened to Kenzie in the past week. What kind of sick publicity stunt—"

A bookstore employee started to move in. Flint held up a hand and cocked his head as his probing eyes scorched Cole. "Can you talk fast?"

Cole blinked. Nodded.

Flint turned to the employee. "I'm going to take a five-minute break." The author smiled at the crowd and stepped away from the table, pulling Cole with him until they reached a couple of empty chairs off to the side.

* * *

"Now," the author said firmly. "Tell me what in the world you're talking about, and do it quick."

Cole spelled it out, pointing to sections in the book as he did.

When he was finished, Flint's mouth had dipped into a deep frown. "You're telling me this really happened—I can verify it with the police?"

"Yes."

"And you came to me because you think I masterminded it?"

"Yes," Cole said again, although if Flint was guilty, he deserved an Oscar.

Flint's brow furrowed. "But wouldn't I be too obvious as a suspect?"

He almost laughed. "In real life, the obvious suspect is usually the right one." Although in this case, that could make it himself. Cole's amusement vanished.

"Touché," Flint said with a wry smile. "I have to get back, but I swear to you, I had nothing to do with it. MacKenzie's okay?"

"She's…spooked, bruised, but okay." Cole studied the author and finally relented, trusting his instincts. "I think whoever it is plans to act out the whole book on her."

Flint shook his head, handed him a card. "I'll see what I can do on my end."

What exactly could Flint do—reprint the novel with a happily-ever-after ending? Maybe he'd let Cole be the hero in the new version. Hey, in fiction, anything could happen.

"Meanwhile, keep me updated. Gotta keep my favorite cover model safe."

The celebrity walked away as the words sank in. Cover model? Cole stiffened. Why hadn't she told him? What—

Then Cole saw Kenzie, threading her way through the

crowd, a purposeful look darkening her pretty face. Looking for him? Cole rose, started toward her.

Then halted as Warren Flint met her gaze and lifted his hand in greeting.

After an awkward greeting from Flint, who studied her with a sharp-eyed gaze, Kenzie excused herself and continued on her path between shelves. To Cole. To safety. She ran a hand along a bookshelf, her steps faltering as she drew closer. Cole stood waiting with crossed arms, narrowed eyes and a stony expression. Prepared for battle.

"So what am I," Cole said as soon as she reached him. "One of those pawns you've been carving? Trying to figure out how to rescue you when it's been a game all along?"

Kenzie halted, the fear draining out of her as confusion took over.

He reached out, gripped her shoulder, glared her full in the face. "Why didn't you tell me that's really you on the cover? What's going on, Kenzie? What does Warren Flint want from you? Is this some screwball publicity stunt?"

Kenzie blinked and shook her head. Was he crazy? Like she would willingly go through all she had been through over the last week... But looking into those intense eyes, she couldn't be angry at him.

"Yes, that's me on the cover. But I don't know what you're talking about. I just picked up my car from the shop and followed you here. You didn't answer your phone and I needed to..."

His face gradually softened. "I'm sorry. Don't know what I was thinking." He touched her shoulder gently. "Do you need help finding a place to stay tonight?"

Kenzie shook her head. "I'll take care of it. But thank you." She could feel the roughness of his thumb, rubbing back and forth against the thin fabric of her blouse. The magnetism in his eyes drew her, even as she told herself to pull back.

"I just want you safe, Kenzie. That's all." He spoke in a hoarse whisper, and she dragged her gaze to his lips. "That's why I'm here. And I'll stay as long as you need me."

Safety. That's all she wanted, too, although right here, right now... Against her better judgment, Kenzie leaned into the strength Cole offered. Snuggled against his chest, with his arms enfolding her, she could block out what her mind was telling her. Listen, instead, to her heart.

"MacKenzie Jacobs."

She loved the way her name sounded on his lips, especially when he spoke into her hair, his breath tickling her scalp.

"You're going to get through this. We'll figure it out." He gave her a squeeze and held her at arm's length.

It was too soon to kiss—she'd only known him, what, a week? But somehow, in this secluded hollow of a crowded bookstore, it seemed like the perfect moment.

Her cell phone rang. Kenzie shook her head regretfully and avoided his gaze as she answered.

"Miss Jacobs," Detective Parker's gruff voice came across the line. "I wanted you to know that you can stay at your house tonight if you'd like. The listening devices are gone, a locksmith has been there already and we're sending patrol cars by at regular intervals."

"Thank you." Kenzie couldn't hold back a shudder.

"There's something else, Miss Jacobs."

Cole had moved closer, a question in his eyes. She forced a smile and held up a finger.

"The sabotage...I know you don't see eye-to-eye with me, but I want you to be careful. So I think there's something you should know."

Slowly pivoting away from her rescuer, Kenzie listened as

the detective told her about another woman, another state, another possible sabotage that had ended in death…and a suspect named Cole Leighton.

Kenzie ended the call. She stayed frozen as Cole stepped beside her, wrapping an arm around her shoulders.

"What was that about?" he said, his eyes aqua pools of innocence.

"Just arranged a place to stay tonight."

"Good." He smiled. " By the way, has anyone ever called you Mac?"

Her head snapped up and she stared at him in horror.

Cole closed his eyes briefly, then bent down until he was at eye level. "Whatever I just said, I'm sorry."

Was he? Or had he just entered the next phase of messing with her life?

She turned and fled.

Kenzie fought tears the whole way home. She should pull over, but she didn't feel safe. Not here, where the dark night closed in on her, in the car that had let her down not so long ago.

Once home, she burst through the door and slammed the new dead bolt in place. She slid down the wall, pressing her face to her knees and wrapped her arms around her head. This was no tornado drill, but *something* was destroying what remained of her heart.

Cole, a bad guy? She didn't want to believe it. Couldn't. But then…

"Has anyone ever called you Mac?"

Yes, but the only person who did had died at the age of thirteen. What she wouldn't do to go back in time, to take back her actions and bring her beloved brother back to life.

But she couldn't.

Kenzie took a deep, shuddering breath. Mikey had never liked it when she cried. He'd tried to make her tough—one reason he'd chosen to call her Mac. Her brother would have wanted her to get over his death.

Maybe she could if she hadn't been the one to cause it.

FOURTEEN

With her feet propped up on a container of bulletin-board supplies, Kenzie flipped through her mail. It was Friday—spring break had been over for barely a week and she was already putting off lesson plans, but maybe there was an important memo she should see right away.

Right.

Kenzie skimmed through a letter from the art teacher, a note about a schedule change and a card from the secretary. At the bottom of the stack rested a manila envelope. She tore off the end and dumped out the contents. Pictures of her students spilled out: Jasmine and Daniel on the seesaw. All of the children in line, walking away from the playground. More photos—close-ups of her and the kids.

Kenzie smiled at one of the snapshots that caught Isaiah with a goofy look on his face, then she flipped through to the bottom of the stack, looking for an explanation. Probably something from the yearbook teacher, or—

One picture caught her eye; wouldn't let go. In the parking lot of the zoo, behind her students' not-so-straight line, was a black van.

Coincidence? Probably. But that didn't stop her heart from jackhammering as she fanned the photographs across her desk.

A black van stood in the background ⌐ ⌐ ⌐ of the photos from the playground. A close-up of her hand on a student's shoulder exposed the still-healing rope burns on Kenzie's wrist.

Her breath came in ragged gasps. Each photo—seemingly innocent, but with a sinister touch. They'd been following her. Stalking her at school. Watching her precious students. Taking photos. And now...

They wanted her to know. Wanted to scare her. Wanted to take things to the next level.

Whatever that was.

The look Kenzie had given him last night had been one full of betrayal and some ancient hurt. And he'd caused it, somehow.

Which was why, just after her school let out, Cole found Kenzie's car in the parking lot and pulled into the space across from it. Juggling a peace offering—a set of wood-carving knives and some chocolates—he made his way up the middle sidewalk to the school's entrance.

In the front office, a secretary studied him through silver-rimmed bifocals and offered a broad smile. "May I help you, sir?"

"I have a delivery for MacKenzie Jacobs."

The secretary checked the clock on the wall. "I think she's still around. Let me see."

She'd just picked up the phone when Kenzie stormed in. Urgency was etched on her face as she dropped her purse and a manila envelope onto the counter.

"Sharon, is Dr. Anderson in?" She seemed not to have noticed Cole's presence.

The secretary glanced from him to Kenzie. "I'll check. Meanwhile, this man—"

"Please, Sharon."

Something was wrong. Again. The strain in her voice was so evident that the secretary apparently forgot about him as well.

"The principal. Right." Sharon spun her chair around and charged through a door behind her.

Cole took a step back as Kenzie drummed her fingertips against the laminate and stared at the closed door. This wasn't the way he'd wanted to approach her—surprise her on her home turf with no warning, when she was already so visibly upset—

Too late. Kenzie shifted, spotted him out of the corner of her eye, then spun to face him full on. "You—"

Sharon returned to her seat in time to postpone whatever accusations were about to spill from Kenzie's grim mouth. "I'm sorry, Kenzie. He must have slipped out the back." Sharon pushed her glasses down on her nose. "Are you okay?"

"I don't know." Kenzie tapped hard against the counter.

Cole backed up another step, giving her more space as tension radiated off of her.

"Anything I can do?" Sharon asked.

One last tap. "Yes. Give him a message to call me ASAP. And…get a sub for me."

Cole fastened his gaze on her. A substitute? Why?

Sharon's frown deepened. "For Monday?"

"Indefinitely."

Before the secretary could react, Kenzie scooped up her belongings and beat a fast retreat, grabbing Cole's arm and hauling him with her.

They dashed to her vehicle in silence. "Talk to me, Kenzie," Cole finally said. "Did something else happen today?"

He tried to remember what happened next in *Obsession,*

but couldn't think clearly. Not when Kenzie seared him with a look, nearly spitting fire as she turned on him.

Probably now was not the time to offer her the wood-carving knives.

Kenzie turned her back on Cole, trying to calm the rage threatening to burst forth. Maybe she should give him the benefit of the doubt. This was America, after all. Innocent until proven guilty. Maybe his claims were true—he'd just fallen into this whole thing and wanted to help. And maybe he hadn't been up to no good back in Texas with Allison what's-her-name—

Yeah, right.

But she still needed to breathe deeply and speak calmly. That way the emergency dispatcher would be able to understand her when she told them to drag Cole Leighton to jail and throw away the key. The dirty, no-good, low-down—

The calm thing wasn't working. Kenzie whirled to face him. "It's been you all along, hasn't it. Stalking me, bugging my house, messing with my car. Taking pictures of my scars, of my *students?*" She got in his face, dug her fingers into his sinewy arm.

He could mess with her—scare her out of her mind. It wasn't that hard to send her cowering into a corner, but this time he'd gone too far. Nobody messed with her kids. No one.

"And now—swooping in here just in time to save me once again. You knew I got those pictures today, didn't you? Because you delivered them yourself." She jerked her hand away from his hot flesh and paced faster. "What kind of telescopic lens do you have, anyway? And where do you hide your van? Or did you just borrow it for the day from your island friend?"

He held up both hands.

No. No more stopping. No more sitting on the sidelines as

a helpless victim, waiting to see what terrible thing would happen next.

"And what about the girl from Texas? Allison, was that her name? Yeah, I heard. Did she die too quickly, and you decided that was no fun, so now…"

Cole's face went deathly white.

The anger whooshed out of Kenzie nearly as fast. She'd gone too far. Whether or not he was the enemy, she'd said too much.

Cole's eyes were nearly closed, blocking access to his thoughts. Without a word, he gently set his packages on the ground, rose and walked away.

Collapsing against the car bumper, Kenzie stared back at the school. Her insides felt as if they had been carved out, leaving her an empty shell.

Was that what she'd just done to Cole?

For the second time in as many days, Kenzie slid behind the wheel and followed Cole. His packages rested on the seat beside her. Chocolate. Wood-carving knives. A card she couldn't bring herself to open.

Between the carefully chosen gifts and the anguished look on his face, Cole had broken through her suspicions. Either her instincts had gone haywire, or Cole Leighton was actually the good guy he seemed to be.

And she'd just shoved his past in his face with no compassion, without knowing the whole story.

She pulled into traffic behind him, tailing him all the way to an apartment complex. Cole was waiting for her when she found a parking space and climbed out of the car.

Heat rushed to Kenzie's face as their eyes met. His were a deeper, darker shade than she remembered. A stormy sea, one that she could drown in if she didn't take care.

What scared her more? The fact that she could be attracted to a psycho? Or that he might not be the enemy…which meant she was back to square one. Kenzie lowered her eyes to the pavement.

"Kenzie…" Cole reached out slowly, like he was trying not to spook a horse. His knuckles scraped her chin lightly, raising her face until she met his gaze once again.

Right now he could probably read her emotions easier than the book he'd given her. The strong attraction. The equally strong distrust. The near hero-worship she tried to keep tamped down. The disgust at what he may have done to her to earn that reaction.

Cole raked a hand through his hair and took a step toward the building. "Let's talk in John's apartment."

Kenzie remained rooted beside her car.

Cole turned back around, his frustration evident. "You're going to have to decide one way or the other, Kenzie. Do you trust me or not? Figure that out, for both our sakes."

She studied every inch of his handsome face. Nothing menacing appeared there. "I want to trust you, but I don't know you, Cole."

"What do you need to know?" His voice was a hoarse whisper.

Who was he? Why was he doggedly persisting in helping her? And what about Detective Parker's suspicions?

But the question that came out was one she didn't want answered. "What about Allison?"

Cole's jaw tensed. Unexpectedly, Kenzie was hit by the urge to run her fingers down his face, maybe kiss away the tension. He was gorgeous. He'd saved her life. A small crush was to be expected, right?

Focus.

Cole moved to sit on a concrete parking stop. After a

long, agonizing silence, he finally spoke. "I didn't take Allison's life. She died in a car wreck. An accident. No matter what Parker said, I had nothing to do with it." Cole's voice took on a ragged edge. "But I did take something I had no right to."

Kenzie leaned against her car, willing herself not to look at him. She heard the pain in his voice. She didn't need to see it written on his face.

"We had an affair." He nearly choked on the word, then let the rest out in a torrent. "Allison and I had been high school sweethearts, but after graduation we went separate ways. She married a military guy. When he was deployed, she came back home. Lived with her parents. I was her friend and confidant, the one who tried to comfort her and fix all her problems. And then things just…went from there. It was brief. Unplanned. So wrong."

He paused, and Kenzie imagined him jabbing his fingers through his hair. Clenching the ends. But still she did not look.

"She was on her way to meet me that night. I was going to call it off. I'd realized—I couldn't live with myself anymore. Allison…she never made it." His voice broke.

In the silence, Kenzie finally dared to turn her head his way. His face was buried in his hands. A man unable to escape his past. Maybe unwilling to.

She understood all too well. Without intending to, Kenzie stretched out her hand, touched his hair, then slid a hand down the muscled arm that had once provided comfort in her dark night. Maybe it was time to return the favor.

"Cole…"

Cole raised his head as Kenzie broke the silence. There was no condemnation on her face. None of the disgust he deserved. Only sadness.

She squeezed his arm, then let go. "So the detective is wrong about your past. I assume he has everything else wrong, too?" No anger lingered in her voice.

"I'm not doing this to you, if that's what you mean. Although I don't know why you should take my word—it's all too bizarre."

"I shouldn't, but I can't help it." Her smile softened the worried lines on her face. "If you aren't my stalker, then that means…what? You risked becoming a suspect just to check out your crazy gut feeling? And you continue helping me— sticking around with the law breathing down your neck and paranoid women throwing things at you—when you could be spending your vacation fishing with your cousin…why?"

Cole stood and turned away from her, jamming his hands in the pocket of his jeans.

"That's okay. I know why." A clack of heels against pavement, then Kenzie's fingers once again warmed his skin. "You're trying to make up for Allison."

Gritting his teeth, Cole remained silent. He could never make up for Allison. Saving Kenzie from the water didn't even out the scales. And now if anything ever happened to her, he'd have something else weighing on his conscience.

But that wasn't the only reason. There was something about Kenzie…

She stepped in front of him. She barely came up to his shoulders, but her gentle touch exuded strength. "You know that's not the way these things work. All you have to do is confess your sins, and God is faithful to forgive them." A hint of another smile tugged at her lips, but it quickly faded. "But I understand. I know what it's like not to be able to forgive yourself."

He saw it in her eyes—a heavy sorrow and regret that mirrored his own. He wanted to comfort her. Wrap her in his arms. Take care of all her problems. Be her…hero.

Instead, he stepped away. Took a deep breath. Uttered a silent prayer.

Once again seeming to understand, Kenzie settled back against the car. "Why don't we count the score as even? A life was lost—accidentally, whether or not you think you were at fault. A life was saved—mine."

"It doesn't work that way." He hadn't just taken one life. He'd ruined Allison's husband's, and he only saw blackness when he looked at his own.

"Maybe not. But there's another way to even the score."

Against his will, Cole's eyes flickered to meet hers.

"A life was lost…on purpose. In your place. To die for your sin." Her expression turned wry. He sensed she wasn't used to preaching, maybe had even surprised herself by doing so.

"I know that. I was raised in church. But I can't help but think…" That his sins were too big…

"That you're not worth it." Kenzie's gaze wouldn't let him go.

Cole didn't respond. Didn't need to, because she'd read his mind.

"I know exactly how you feel."

Cole turned away once again and stared toward the road. "How could you?" A Christian school teacher, probably as innocent as her students.

A long pause, then, "Because someone once died for me."

Her words—sad and whispery soft—immobilized him, but something else altogether made his blood run cold.

Across the lot, a man sat in the driver's seat of a silver sedan.

FIFTEEN

She was ready to spill her heart. Open up and tell someone all about Mikey, how much she'd loved him, and how much she wished it had been she that died that night, leaving the beloved child on earth for her parents to dote on.

Instead, Cole's back stiffened. He uttered a gruff, "Let's go," and Kenzie found herself following close on his heels as he pulled her toward his car.

"Did you see something?" The street appeared normal. No sinister strangers roaming the sidewalks. No one in a ski mask or driving a black van. "What's going on?"

"Maybe nothing. Get in."

He backed out of the parking space before her seat belt clicked home. Urgency was still written on his expression, but his driving didn't show it. Slow and steady, he drove through the lot and down the street. Stopped at the corner just a moment too long. Glanced briefly into the mirror, then made his turn.

"Where are we going?"

"I don't know." Cole sped up, glancing again at the mirror.

This time, the move caused what felt like tiny insects to crawl under her skin. She looked in her own mirror and saw a sedan a few car-lengths behind them. Farther back, a police cruiser just made the turn.

"Which one are you running from?" She should trust him by now. She *did* trust him. But somehow it just seemed easier—and so much harder—to blame the man she was with.

"Do you recognize the silver car?"

"I don't think so. Should I?"

Cole let out a sigh. "I don't know. It could be nothing. But in the book…"

The insects swarmed this time, and Kenzie rubbed her arms hard. "In the book, what?"

"A silver Lincoln Town Car followed the heroine around. I'm going to see how far he follows us. It could be nothing— an undercover cop or just someone who happens to be going the same way we are."

The cop car made another turn, disappearing from view. The sedan inched closer. Kenzie kept her head facing forward, but her eyes remained on the side mirror. "I can't see his face." Not that it would matter. She'd have to get close enough to see a scar, and that wasn't going to happen if she could help it.

Then again, maybe that would be the only way to catch them: live bait.

Her breath caught, and suddenly she couldn't fill her lungs again. The day darkened until a sharp pain on her arm made her gasp for breath.

"Breathe, Kenzie."

She jerked her head up and found Cole trying to watch both her and the road as he drove onto the ramp to I-85.

"You okay now?"

Rubbing the spot where he'd pinched her, she didn't answer. Only focused once again on the vehicle in the mirror. Would they stalk her for the rest of her life—scare her away from jobs and friends until she was alone and terrified and ready to have them end the game for her?

No way. MacKenzie Jacobs may be scared of the dark and of storms and whatever else, but she would not spend her lifetime cowering.

"Stop the car."

"What?" Cole sent her a sidelong look.

"I want to see if it's them." Quick, before she lost her nerve.

"So do I, but—"

Heat bubbled up and spilled out. "Right now!" Her eyes burned as she grabbed for the door handle.

"Kenzie. No." Cole spoke calmly, but he reached for the automatic lock button. "I want to get him as much as you, but you can't just hop out of the car and flag the driver down."

He was right, of course, but she didn't want to admit it. "So what do you suggest, Sherlock?"

Cole didn't react to the venom in her voice. "I just want to make sure he's really following us. We'll call Parker. He probably put a GPS tracker on my car anyway—"

Kenzie shot him a quick look and caught a flash of emotion cross his face. Chagrin? Annoyance? Something flickered inside her—a longing to be able to read him, to know him from the inside out. She squelched it.

Cole kept talking. "So they'll be able to find us. And then we'll confront him."

It could be over soon. A phone call. A squealing of brakes, flashing of red-and-blue lights, and a man led away in handcuffs. Or…

"Cole, did this happen in the book? How did the scene turn out?" Did she really want to know? If Monique ended up locked in a closet somewhere…

Cole checked the mirror, and Kenzie's eyes followed his. They still had a tail. Farther back now. They changed lanes, then Cole clicked on the blinker and took the next exit. "Call Parker. He's still on us."

Kenzie picked up her phone, dialed and held it to her ear, no longer wanting to know the answer to her questions. If it was that bad…

It didn't matter, because it wasn't going to happen. But still, she should have read the stupid book.

The detective promised someone would be there as quickly as possible. Kenzie hung up but kept the phone clutched tightly in one hand. The other braced against the door as Cole whipped into a U-turn.

"What's going on?" Kenzie turned to look behind them. A red Pontiac. A tan SUV. Where was—

"He ditched us."

"So you're doing *what?*"

Cole didn't have to answer, as they were fast approaching the rear end of a silver Town Car. The hunted becoming the hunters—there was some sort of poetic justice about that. If they didn't get pulled over for speeding or get their windshield shot out.

"See if you can get the license number, Zee."

Kenzie blinked. Zee? Biting back an amused smile, she strained to read the license. Most of it was covered in mud. She jotted down what she could and tapped it into a text message for Detective Parker. "Now what?" They'd followed the sedan into an industrial area. "Please tell me you know what you're doing."

"I have no idea what I'm doing."

"This wasn't in the book?"

"Are you kidding?"

"I thought you said the Town Car was in there. Which is why we're here. Doing…whatever we're doing."

"There was. But Monique only saw it following her. She tried to shake him off a couple times. It worked, she thought."

So nothing horrific happened with the Town Car. That was

good. Then again… "So she didn't exactly go chasing it through unfamiliar neighborhoods with the policemen not yet in sight?"

"Not exactly."

"Ah." A tremor shook her. From fear or excitement? Kenzie rubbed her clammy hands together. They were going to get this guy. With Cole at the wheel, she could somehow believe that.

The sedan sped up once again. Cole spun around a corner, maneuvered through a parking lot, went too fast through an intersection. But when he turned onto a side street, their prey was gone.

"What—?"

As they idled in the center of a deserted street, the sound of a siren caught up to them. Cole smirked. "Guess I was right about the tracking device."

"Good thing." Kenzie looked around a street lined with run-down warehouses and deserted parking lots, graffiti and broken windows. "Because I don't have a clue where we are. You?"

"Nope."

"And you promise this scene isn't in the book?" Like where the hero was shot and the heroine dragged to a deserted warehouse where she was used to test the newest biological weapon?

"It's not in the book." His smile melted her fears.

"Okay. One more question."

A police officer strode toward them, talking into his radio. "Go ahead."

She studied his face—the blue-green eyes sparkling with lingering excitement from the car chase, the broad lips curled in an exhilarated smile, the scruffy jaw and determined chin and long lashes and…what was her question again?

Oh. Right. "Did you really call me Zee?"

His smile widened. "Do you mind?"

She tipped her head to the side, trying to decide.

His eyes flickered, softened. Gently, he curled his hand around the back of her neck and drew her closer. She felt the heat of his gaze down to her toes as he searched her face for permission.

She licked her lips, and his mouth claimed hers. Just for one wonderful moment, then he pulled away and trailed a finger down her cheek and across her lips.

No, she didn't mind at all.

SIXTEEN

Obsession.

Cole typed the title into a search engine and glanced over at Kenzie. She sat beside him, sprawled in one of John's dining-room chairs, reading the book. He doubted the thriller was her typical choice for light Saturday reading, but she seemed relaxed enough. The scents of her shampoo and perfume mixed together to create a heady fragrance, and he had to force his attention back to the computer.

"Hey, Zee, has Flint been in touch yet?" He tried not to smile as Kenzie reacted as she had every time so far—she blinked, hesitated as if deciding whether he was actually talking to her and then swallowed a bemused grin.

"He left a message, checking to see how I was doing. What did you say to him, anyway?"

"I accused him of acting out his book on you as a publicity stunt."

Kenzie laughed. "Really? How'd that go?"

Cole shrugged as he skimmed the descriptions of various Web sites the search had pulled up. Interviews, reviews, Amazon.com…nothing looked interesting. What had he expected to find? He'd scoured the book almost enough to quote it. The reviewers couldn't have caught much that he hadn't already. But maybe there was some sort of fan site that could yield some clues. The gunmen had to be obsessed fans.

"Wait." Kenzie leaned closer.

Cole closed his eyes, trying not to think about the sweet curve of her lips, the way her mouth had felt against his yesterday.

"What's that one?"

Focus, focus. Cole looked where she pointed. Something on YouTube. He clicked and, as the video loaded, read the description: "Me and a friend, acting out part of *Obsession* by Warren Flint."

While the clip came alive, Kenzie seemed to do the opposite. Her hand, lying next to his on the computer desk, stiffened with her fingers outstretched. Even before the voice sounded from the tinny speakers, tension radiated from her body.

As Atlanta traffic rushed by, the man behind the camera explained how his friend had adapted the book for a screenplay, and they were going to rehearse their roles. His voice did sound familiar. Maybe. But Cole doubted he could confidently identify it.

Then the screen cut to a backwoods road. Kenzie grabbed Cole's hand. He watched, open-mouthed, as a bound and blindfolded Kenzie appeared on the screen, and a second man wearing a ski mask transferred her to the trunk of a waiting car—a silver Lincoln Town Car. The masked man sat in the driver's seat, started the vehicle and drove away, leaving the first man at the scene. Then, while sharing how excited he was about this project and how talented the girl was, the man behind the camera drove the van deeper into the woods…and deserted it.

The clip ended with a promise of more "sneak peeks" to come. Their next rehearsal was scheduled for Monday.

They sat in silence for a moment, then Kenzie hit Replay. While she watched it again, Cole dialed Parker's cell phone.

Kenzie gripped Cole's hand as the clip played again. His voice faded. The lights dimmed. Everything was shoved to the background as the screen pulled her in. Closer. Back in time to that forest where she thought her life was about to end.

Watching herself stumble, she jerked in her seat. When the man with the leather jacket held the gun to her head, she felt chilled at the memory of the cold metal. The trunk popped open, and she tightened her ankles around the chair legs as the Kenzie on the monitor was lifted and dumped inside. That's when he'd slammed the gun against her head so hard—

A hand cupped her face. She flinched, blinked, saw Cole and his black polo blocking her line of vision.

"Kenzie, you're okay now. We're going to get him."

His hand was warm, strong, gentle. His eyes—reassuring and full of empathy with a flicker of righteous anger. The man was a fixer. He yearned to help, and he was good at it. That's what made him great; that's what she loved about him, what made her want to kiss him until they were both breathless…

And that's what had made him fall.

She drew back, not sure what to do with that.

Cole took the hint and dropped his hand. "Parker is getting some guys on it right away—they'll go through the system to get permission to trace that post. You can't see the plate on the Lincoln, but another team will try to track down the van. Maybe they can get some prints, run the tags, all that jazz."

"So…we're getting close?"

A slow smile spread across his face. His lips curved higher on the left side, giving him a roguish look. "We're getting close."

A lock of hair fell across his forehead; Kenzie clenched

her hands to keep from pushing it back. "So they could catch him. Before Monday."

"Maybe even today."

Air whooshed out of her body in a long sigh. Sweet relief. "I won't need to look over my shoulder to see if someone's following me? Or finish reading that stupid book? I can go back to my job? See my kids?"

"Almost. Not yet."

Of course not. She wouldn't be able to totally relax until the two men were sentenced to rot in prison. But it was nice to dream…like she was doing right now, gazing at Cole with him gazing back.

"So what do you want to do until Parker calls back?"

She tried not to stare at his mouth—glanced at the ceiling and back down, then watched as his lips curved once again. She wanted to trace that smile with her fingers. Feel his warm mouth take hers once again, shiver in delight instead of fear.

Instead, she sat on her hands and looked away. "Let's…order a pizza. And while we gorge ourselves on a celebratory meal, you can tell me everything about yourself and then maybe I'll teach you to whittle." Which would keep her hands busy so she wouldn't remember how kissable he was…

Oh, she was headed toward a whole different kind of trouble.

"Pizza it is. The rest is negotiable. After all, you already know…well, a lot about me. And I know next to nothing about you."

"I like extra cheese and mushrooms." She looked up at him, catching the appreciative glint in his eyes. "There. That's my order for the afternoon. Your turn."

"My turn…" He reached for the mouse, minimized the screen recording her day of horror and called up a new search. Papa John's. Perfect. "I like the Works. But I think we can compromise if we add green peppers."

Kenzie tilted her head, then gave a quick nod, trying to maintain a somber expression.

"Good," he said with a smirk. A few clicks of the mouse and he finished their order.

She loved how he played along. He'd indulge her this afternoon. Tell her whatever she wanted to know, play whatever game she had in mind in order to keep her from worrying about what was going down at the station. The drama would be over soon, which meant Cole might head home…

A sharp pang stole her breath away. She didn't want him to leave. She wanted to know his heart, and she wanted him to know hers. That scared her more than the video clip had, maybe even more than being left for dead in a deserted boathouse.

She forced a cheery note into her voice. "Favorite candy bar, color, and book of the Bible."

"I like Reese's—can't go wrong with peanut butter and chocolate. And I like the color blue." He looked into her eyes and winked. "My favorite book of the Bible…well, I guess it would have to be the Psalms."

Kenzie cleared her throat and looked away. "The Psalms, huh?" She could understand that—she'd cried the words of David more than once herself.

When he made no reply, she glanced at him again. His face had reddened. He busied his hands, flipping through his wallet to find money for the pizza. It took a moment, but the reason for his embarrassment hit home.

"Cole, I'm not judging you for your past. What you did was wrong. You've admitted as much. But I'm not filtering everything you say or do through that."

"You didn't automatically think of the verses about being washed white as snow?"

"No." She wanted to touch him, to show him he was no longer unclean. But he had to accept that first, see it for himself. Funny, how she could see exactly how to fix his God issues and had no idea what to do about her own. "Actually, I was thinking how much some of those Psalms have meant to me, as well."

Gently, he tugged her fingers into his cupped palm. "Thank you, Zee."

Closing her eyes for a brief moment, she savored the sound of the nickname and the feel of her hand being held by both of his. "You're welcome." The atmosphere was too heavy. Too…personal. She didn't have the fortitude to deal with Cole's issues and her own while wondering if the cops had caught her stalkers.

Slowly, she withdrew her hand and cast her gaze around the room, looking for a distraction. She spotted a sketchbook nearby and reached for it, absently stroking the cover before flipping it open.

Pencil drawings filled the pages. Kenzie flipped through, slowing down as she reached the last of them.

Cole's hand gently tapped the page, and he wore a grimace as Kenzie met his eyes. "I'm not very good at drawing people. I just do it when I need a break from work or something."

She blinked. "These are yours?"

He shrugged.

"You don't have to be embarrassed. They're really good."

Among shadowy landscapes and bridge designs, there were also soft images of a woman. She felt a pang of…something. Was the woman Allison?

"Of course," she forced her tone to stay light, "I work with first-graders, so what do I know?"

Kenzie dropped her gaze back to the sketchbook. What she did know was that the last drawing was of a woman cradled close to a man's chest. The same way Cole had held her when he'd saved her from the water.

He was getting too close. If something happened to him, she wouldn't be strong enough to bring him to safety.

Cole could sense her withdrawing as she left the computer desk and curled up in a corner of the couch. He spoke up to pull her back as much as to distract her attention from the drawings. He hadn't meant for her to see those.

"So how did you get into whittling?" The work in her home had been amazing, not that he knew anything about carving.

Shutters closed over her expression. Cole groaned inwardly as Kenzie reached for her purse.

"Wait. We can drop the subject. Or I can take you somewhere if you'd rather not stay, but you need to be with someone until the cops—"

A faint smile broke through her obvious pain. "No. It's okay. I was just going to show you this." She pulled a pocketknife from the purse and set it on the coffee table. "I had an older brother—he was the one who used to call me Mac. This was his. He carried it with him everywhere—sharpened sticks to roast marshmallows, carved his girlfriends' initials into trees... He'd even started trying to make dollhouse furniture for me before he died. Although he used different tools for that."

Cole studied her as she rubbed the worn handle. "You picked up whittling to honor his memory?"

"Yeah. If that makes any sense." Her eyes shone with liquid pain.

"Absolutely." He reached for her hand. "You two were obviously very close."

Stroking her arm, he couldn't help noticing how soft her skin was compared to the roughness of his own. A symbol of how they differed. MacKenzie Jacobs—soft, sensitive, vulnerable. Cole Leighton—rough around the edges, marred, calloused.

Avoiding her eyes, he pulled back. He could make her laugh. Protect her. Feed her. Whatever. But there was nothing he could do to deserve the love of someone like her. He'd thought that at some point he would have redeemed himself enough to deserve another chance.

But he couldn't. So where did that leave him?

SEVENTEEN

The pizza man delivered right on time. Kenzie waved Cole on, then covered her eyes with one hand. She left the other hand where it was, just in case Cole wanted to reach for it again when he returned.

He didn't. Probably because he didn't trust himself. *Father, he is so stubborn. Can You please show him he doesn't have to be the man he once was? Help him get over it already?*

The aroma of spicy marinara and bread wafted into the room. Kenzie kept her eyes closed. Mikey had loved pizza. He'd always traded his mushrooms for her crusts. Now she threw the crusts away.

He'd been gone for so many years. It wasn't natural for grief to last this long. She should be over it by now, but the guilt made that impossible. Kenzie and Cole, both hung up on their pasts. Living their quiet, background lives, eaten up by guilt. No wonder they were so drawn to each other.

Or at least, she was drawn to him. Did he feel it, too? Yesterday's kiss had seemed to say so, but maybe that had just been a result of high emotion—the excitement of the car chase or something.

"Ready to eat?" Cole's eyes searched hers. "Or you want to talk some more first?"

"Let's eat." Stuffing her face with food might keep her from crying, because suddenly she yearned to spill the whole story. Lay it all out there. Start the mending process, if healing was even possible.

Kenzie settled at the table with a plate and a bottle of cream soda. After an awkward pause, Cole bowed his head and prayed for the meal and the investigation. A humble and heartfelt prayer. So…he still believed. He still prayed. He just didn't think he was worthy of an answer—for himself, at least.

Well, that sounded familiar. Maybe they should pray on each other's behalf. God might listen then.

"My parents adored my brother. He was always happy. Mowed the yard without complaint. Made good grades and lots of friends." She took a bite of the pizza and chewed, hardly tasting it. "Mikey was one of those guys who just wanted everyone to be happy, and he'd do whatever he could to make it happen. My parents doted on him."

She twisted off the bottle cap and took a swig, trying to wash down the lump in her throat.

"But…they didn't dote on you?"

"Oh, they didn't need to." She said it quickly, not meeting his eyes. He saw too much. "They adored Mikey, and he adored me. No problem."

"Until he was gone."

Determined not to say any more, she choked down more pizza. Her silence must have said enough.

"They blamed you?"

"*I* blame me. Mikey was babysitting me. There was a tornado. He got me into the basement. I—I was scared and crying for my favorite doll, trying to go after it. He told me it was too dangerous, but I was inconsolable."

Biting her lip, she fought the tears that threatened to fall. "He finally disappeared up the steps to go get it. Shut the door behind him. It was so dark. There was a roaring sound. Things crashing. And…and Mikey never came back. When the storm—" She choked on the word. The storm. The one that still caused her to cower in fear when thunder rumbled. The sorrow poured out in racking sobs as Cole's arms closed around her. His warmth warded off the chill caused by the horrific pictures her memory called up in vivid detail. Of their home in ruins. Her dollhouse and the tiny furnishings demolished. Mikey's body, thrown like the rag doll he'd been trying to rescue.

She buried her face in Cole's broad shoulder, wetting his shirt with her tears. How could she have been so selfish? Begging Mikey to leave safety. And now what was she doing? Spilling her guts to an incredibly handsome and hurting man. Soaking up his comfort and toying with the idea of falling in love with him. Looking at him as Mr. Fix-It, her hero, while someone played deadly cat-and-mouse games with her. True, Parker might be taking down one of the gunmen. But what about the other? The one with a charming voice and the stone heart of a killer?

Cole Leighton would do anything to help her. It was who he was, his gift and his curse. And if she let him act as her protector…he was going to wind up dead. Like Mikey. She knew it with a cold certainty.

Kenzie pulled back and gazed into Cole's face. His eyes were more green now than blue, and damp with pain for her. She touched his scratchy jaw, then let her hand fall to his chest and felt the rapid beat of his heart, its rhythm matching the hard pounding of her own. She could love this man. And the people she loved got hurt.

No. Not this time.

* * *

Cole felt Kenzie retreating even further before she moved from his side. Those expressive eyes of hers told all. Now he knew why she was afraid of the dark and of storms, but something had just scared her once again, even in the brightly lit apartment. Did she still think he was behind this whole thing? Or—a weight landed in his stomach, dragging his heart down as far as it could go—did she think he was attempting to seduce her?

She stood in front of him, leaned down to plant a sweet, chaste kiss on his cheek, then trailed a hand down his arm and backed away. "Thanks for lunch."

All two bites she'd managed to eat.

"And for listening."

Her gaze shifted away from him. Probably trying to come up with an excuse to leave—something that would make him believe she had to go, but that she was okay and would be safe. No excuse would convince him of that.

She apparently figured that out. "I have to go now."

"What did I do, Zee?"

"Nothing." A belated tear slipped down her cheek, but she looked him firmly in the eye. "You're perfect, okay?" She gave him a believe-me-or-else glare she must have practiced on her students. "There's just something I have to do."

"Let me call someone—"

Before he could stop her, she was out the door, purse slung over her shoulder, keys held tightly in her hand.

Kenzie felt Cole's stare as she strode down the hallway toward the elevator. Reaching it, she pushed the button hard. Then punched it again, willing it to arrive before she gave in and ran back to his arms.

Please, God, don't let Cole think I'm running from him.

She was, but not for any reason he would come up with. *Heal his heart. Help him to see that his punishment has already been taken care of, that all he has to do is accept it.*

The heavy door slid open. Empty. Kenzie stepped inside, turned and met Cole's eyes. He stood just outside the apartment door, leaning one arm against the door frame, wearing a torn expression. Then the elevator door clanged shut.

Kenzie hit the button for the bottom floor. As long as Cole could find her, he wouldn't give up trying to keep her safe. And that would put him in danger. Which meant she needed to do what she probably should have done in the first place.

Disappear.

Cole ended his call with Parker just as John entered the apartment.

"Where's Kenzie?" John set his briefcase on the table, and his eyebrows furrowed as he studied the nearly full pizza box. "I thought you were going to stick with her until—"

"She left. Out of the blue. I don't know what happened."

"Is she safe?"

Cole threw the phone onto the couch. "I have no idea. She's not answering my calls. Parker's going to send someone to check on her...if he can find her. I swear I have no idea what I did." He jabbed his fingers through his hair, barely registering its length.

"Maybe you didn't do anything. Maybe *she* had something she had to do."

"Like what? She's not working right now. If she needed to talk to Parker, she could have called him. And—"

"What's this?" John picked up a pocketknife and waved it slightly.

"Kenzie's brother's knife." Cole took it, turned it over in his hands. Kenzie would want it, wherever she was.

"She has a brother?"

"Had. He died when she was little. She thinks it's her...fault..." Cole closed the knife in his fist. "You don't suppose..." Yes, he did. Kenzie was ditching him. Not because of anything he'd said, but because she was afraid of what could happen to him. She'd rather be vulnerable than put him at risk.

If the knife weren't so precious to her, he'd jam it into the wall. Instead, Cole let out a roar of frustration. She had become more to him than a duty. More than a way to try to even out his life's scales. He barely knew her, but their spirits had touched. Didn't she know he didn't want to be protected? That he'd do anything to help her? That it would kill him if she got hurt? He would trade his life for hers, if she would just let him.

Cole remembered her face. Her voice. Then her words. *A life was lost...on purpose. In your place.*

The memory sliced sharply, deep into his heart. Cole wasn't the only one who'd been rejected. *Jesus, what have I done?*

EIGHTEEN

As soon as the plane leveled off, Kenzie pulled *Obsession* from her carry-on bag and put it on the tray table. She stared at the cover—at her face, contorted with a horror she hadn't had to dig too deeply to feel during the photo shoot. That could be her in real life. Two days—that's all they had until the next "rehearsal." If the video clip didn't come through for them, the only other way to find the guys was if they came after her again.

This time, she'd be ready…she hoped. Detective Parker had told her they were going to shut her kidnappers down.

If he didn't, the kidnappers were going to shut her down. Maybe forever.

No. Kenzie tapped the book. She had the blueprint. If she could employ some of the same out-of-the-box creativity she used to come up with lesson plans, she could figure out a way to beat the gunmen at their own game, to turn the mouse into a tiger.

Or just staying alive would work, too. Warren Flint's heroine had as many problems as she did. If nothing else, reading the story would help her focus on someone else's problems, figure out how to make sure they didn't become her own.

She set notepaper on the tray table and flipped to the back of the book…because the end was all that really mattered.

Last page. Monique, walking down a deserted road in the middle of the night. Away from her captors—what, she got taken again? Kenzie gritted her teeth and skimmed the rest of the page. Monique was finally free.

And then she found herself framed by headlights…

The end.

Oh, that was a lot of help. Friend or foe—you'll never know. What an incredibly horrible ending. And it had been a blockbuster hit?

The only plan that scene had led to was to stay off the road. Brilliant. She'd have to go back further to find the part where she learned how not to be abducted again in the first place. Skimming another page, she skipped over a scene at Monique's work—an upscale restaurant. Monique quit when she got a package with pictures of her coworkers—yet another déjà vu moment.

Obsession had lost its creepiness. Now the whole thing just made her mad. She swallowed a growl and read.

> *Three grocery sacks should be all Monique needed to change her life. She could load them into her suitcase, leave her car near a bus station and ride to the end of the line. No shadows would chase her. No more hang-up phone calls or silver sedans. A new home, new job, new start.*
>
> *Hair dye. Lighter makeup. Clothes a couple sizes too big. Reading glasses. Sunglasses. A book about computers. She could get a job as a receptionist—it couldn't be that much different than her former hostess position.*

Monique threw the items into her cart and added more. The faster she went, the more she felt watched. Could the other customers tell she was changing her identity? Did they see her tossing glances over her shoulder, peeking around corners, suddenly ducking into aisles? Did they notice anyone following her, or did they only see a paranoid woman with wild eyes and a face haunted by fear?

No more. This would end tonight when she boarded that bus—a slightly plump honey-blonde with a shy smile who went by the name M.J.

Monique paid in cash. No trips to an ATM to tip off her stalker that she was about to run. She'd take what she had on hand and worry about the rest later. Much later, when she was no longer worrying about staying alive.

Kenzie tapped her pencil against the page. Why couldn't she do that? Was she not brave enough to drop everything and leave? Oh, sure, she'd just done that, but only for a couple of days, and heading to her mother's home didn't really count. What had Warren Flint said about Monique? About herself? That they had an inner strength they weren't even aware of?

Well, she might have been the author's inspiration, but he'd used his imagination for that part. Kenzie wasn't strong, because she couldn't let her life go. Her home, her job, her church… It wasn't much, but it was who she was. What she was comfortable with. What she loved.

MacKenzie Jacobs was no Monique.

Kenzie wasn't at home. Detective Parker hadn't heard from her. Neither had her school. Cole's calls were going straight to voice mail. He hadn't been around her long enough to know her favorite haunts.

He'd even called her mother in Kansas. Eleanor Jacobs remembered who he was. She kindly informed him that she hadn't heard from Kenzie, but would let him know if she did.

Just in case she'd forgotten, he called her again. "Mrs. Jacobs, this is Cole."

"Still no word from MacKenzie?" For the first time she spoke with a note of concern.

"No, ma'am. You?" But he already knew the answer.

"Not yet. But she'll be fine. She's always been an independent person, and she loves her privacy…" Eleanor cleared her throat, probably thinking if she made her voice sound stronger, her words would be more convincing. "I'm sure there's no reason to worry. But would you have her give me a call when she does turn up?"

Cole agreed and disconnected, then continued to sit in Kenzie's driveway, wishing she would magically appear before him. Or that Detective Parker would call and let him know he had the suspects in custody. If she was trying to shake him, she'd succeeded. But she'd done more than that— she'd scared him half to death.

The seconds ticked by, agonizingly slow. The driveway remained empty. Cole kept his eyes open, focusing on the house, refusing to give in to the horrific mental pictures forming.

Why had he let her walk away?

Jesus, You gave Your life for mine. Forgive me for turning my back on Your sacrifice. He had caught a taste of what that felt like. *I know I don't deserve Your forgiveness, but I understand now.*

If Kenzie was still alive—if he had the chance again, saving her wouldn't be about anything she had done. It would be about who she was.

Beloved.

* * *

Kenzie needed a break. From the book, the plane, the fellow passengers who seemed to be staring at her with sinister intent. Maybe she just needed a break from life. She wanted to curl up under the cottonwood tree at Mom's and whittle something. Like Cole. But she'd left Mikey's knife at John's apartment and the rest of her tools at home. What had she been thinking?

That she needed to get away before it was too late. Not because Cole was going to kill her or anything—no, she trusted him with her life, and that was the problem. He was making her fall in love, and she didn't know what to do with that. Someone was going to get hurt through all of this. She hoped it would be her, because she couldn't live with herself if she caused Cole more pain...or worse.

You already hurt him.

So she had. But she'd left him—he was out of harm's way now. That was all that mattered.

Or was it?

Here she was, on a plane headed to...her *mother's?* No one had seemed to follow her to the airport. But then, Monique had run, and somehow—Kenzie hadn't read far enough to know the specifics—she'd ended up abducted once again. If they figured out where she was going—and really, how hard could that be?—another family member could die because of her.

The plane touched down in Wichita. Too late to back out now.

"She's here," Mrs. Jacobs said.

Relief poured through Cole as he switched the phone to his left hand and grabbed his suitcase. "When?"

"She walked through the door maybe ten minutes ago. The shock of my life, let me tell you."

"She's all right?" There was a long pause as Cole rummaged through his things. A change of clothes, his cell-phone charger—

"She's fine. Just...quiet. Of course, she usually is. Tell me, Cole, did you hurt my daughter?"

The knot in his chest tightened once more, and Cole's hand stilled on his shaving kit. "Not that I know of, ma'am."

"Then what's going on? Because my daughter never comes home."

"I'm sure she'll fill you in. Thank you for letting me know she's okay." He disconnected and ran for the car. He had a plane to catch.

She shouldn't have come to Kansas. Kenzie knew it the instant she walked through the doors of her mother's home. Her parents had rebuilt on the same property after they'd lost the house in the tornado. The same floor plan. They'd even set up Mikey's room almost like it had been right before he died.

It helped keep their memories of him alive. It had kept her nightmares active. To get to her old bedroom, she had to pass a window. If she looked out, she'd be able to see the place where Mikey's body had been found.

She didn't look.

Her mother followed her and set a stack of clean towels on the bed.

"Why don't you move to Georgia, Mom? We could find you a cute little house or maybe a duplex. Easier for you to keep up with." Closer to her only family left. Maybe they'd finally learn to get along.

"Oh, I couldn't stand the traffic. And I couldn't leave your father and your brother."

Both long dead and buried, but still her priorities. Go figure.

"Well…think about it."

Kenzie began to unpack, and her mother settled on the edge of the bed. She talked about the town gossip. The price of milk. How she was looking at getting a new dining-room table, and if Mikey were alive today, he could have turned his woodworking passion into a lucrative furniture business. Might have gone nationwide, and taken them all to Hawaii on his Christmas bonus. Oh, and they were invited to the neighbor's house at eight for dessert.

Through the open curtains, Kenzie watched as rain fell in sheets and the sky gradually darkened, deepening the shadows in the room. Her mother finally left, and Kenzie sighed in relief.

Now what? She could run away—settle in whatever small friendly town hit her fancy. Do whatever she had to do to shed this nightmare.

Then again, she'd been trying to run from nightmares all her life. Where had that gotten her? To a city she feared, a job that could be in jeopardy and a duplex she spent all her free time holed up in, attempting to whittle away her guilt with her brother's old pocketknife.

It was time to stand on her own two feet and face the enemy, come what may. She'd already faced death twice. Maybe she had the luck of a cat with its nine lives.

Or maybe the third time would be the charm.

Kenzie's lips settled into a grim line. She'd finish reading, make some notes, come up with that elusive plan. Then she'd go back and end this thing. Alone.

I am with you always.

Kenzie grimaced as the verse popped into her mind. Leaning against the top of the iron headboard, she turned her face to the ceiling. *Are You really? Because I'm not feeling it.*

The thought had been suppressed for so long, and both

relief and guilt flooded her as she allowed it to be directed to Someone other than herself. It was irreverent to question the Almighty God. But she might die in a few days. It was past time to have this heart-to-heart.

She stared at the popcorn texture that made the white paint appear dingy. *You created me, You sent Your Son to die for my salvation, You forgave me when I asked…but that's the extent of our relationship, isn't it? Do my thoughts even make it past the ceiling?*

The tears welled, but Kenzie choked them down. She continued in a broken whisper. "Is it so awful to ask to be loved? Not to be the favorite one or anything, but…can someone love me just because of who I am? Could Mom love me for no other reason than that I'm her child? Not just accept me—*love* me."

Cole's face rose in front of her, but she shut it down, wincing. She lowered her head and cupped her chin in her hands. Her selfishness had made an appearance once again. People who loved her died. She knew that by now. Mikey, with the tornado. Dad, with his heart attack. Loving MacKenzie Jacobs posed a dangerous risk.

Yet she yearned for it. To have someone who made it a point to know things about her—that yes, she was twenty-six and still slept with a light on, so please don't flip the switch when you leave the room. And she carried her brother's knife everywhere she went because it made her feel like a part of him was still with her. That she was still…loved.

But she'd lost Mikey's knife. She'd never had her mother's love. And God wasn't listening. Again.

The knot in Kenzie's throat gradually loosened. No more tears fell. She sat quietly in the night, listening for God to answer. Nothing.

Just eight long gongs from the grandfather clock.

Her mother tapped on the door and opened it. "You about ready?"

Kenzie studied her mother. Eleanor Jacobs was aging gracefully. An attractive sixtysomething-year-old, she could probably date any widower in town. But she didn't. She lived in the lonely past.

Maybe they had more in common than Kenzie first thought. For a brief moment, Kenzie wanted to ask if they could skip going next door and curl up on the king-size bed in the master bedroom, watch a comedy and fall asleep. Together against the dark.

The phone rang. Kenzie checked her hair in the mirror while her mother scooped up the handset on the nightstand.

"Hello. Jacobs residence."

A long pause. Kenzie slipped on her shoes.

"Is anyone there?"

Bent over her laces, Kenzie went still. *No. Please, no.*

"Hello?" her mother said again, waited a moment longer, then hung up. "Must be a bad connection—just some weird ticking noise. Let's go, dear. I hear Needa made cherry cheesecake."

Mom flipped a switch and the room plunged into blackness.

NINETEEN

Cole had already read *Obsession*, already stressed over every scene, wondering if Kenzie would end up in the same predicaments, feel the same emotions as Monique. But, as the plane winged its way to Kansas, he leaned the book against the window beside him and tried to find where Kenzie's stalkers had left off.

He flipped through, found where Monique fled her home and changed her identity. Did Kenzie even know how closely she'd followed in the heroine's footsteps? Stuffing down the thought, he read through the next scene.

> *No lens could see through the thick drapes that kept the hotel room in semi-darkness. Still, Monique sensed someone watching. Waiting. Laughing.*
>
> *No one had followed her here. She was in a new town, she was a new person. She should be able to begin again. Everyone wanted a fresh start at some point.*
>
> *But not everyone had to leave behind the man they loved.*

Cole's eyes caught on those words, surprised to find himself hoping this one line would turn out to be true. Did Kenzie regret leaving him behind? Could she possibly fall in love with him?

How could she? She knew his past.

Curling up on the bed, Monique hugged a pillow, allowing herself to grieve what she was giving up. But only a moment. There were things to do. Plans to make and set into motion.

Monique moved to the bathroom and set her bag on the counter. Her hair had already been altered to a warm blonde. She pulled scissors from her bag, hesitated a moment, then cut long bangs before braiding the rest of her hair. Next, makeup. She willed her hands steady and worked to apply it. Lighter foundation to hide her olive skin tone. A little extra blush to add color so she didn't look as scared as she felt. The dark shadows under her eyes showed through, but she let them be.

Altogether, the hairstyle, baggy jeans and sweater, and the makeup worked to give her a slightly harried soccer-mom look. Monique the polished hostess of Chef Jean's was nowhere to be seen, except in the eyes. Colored contacts would make the transformation complete. She made a note to find some before her next hotel stop.

She moved to the desk and opened her laptop. A file was minimized on her screen. Puzzled, she opened the document. Bold letters blinked from the screen.

You can run but you cannot hide.

Reaching up, Cole adjusted a knob, closing off the flow of cold air. But the coldness came from inside. Flint had written the novel from a single viewpoint—Monique's. He didn't have to explain how everything happened; it wasn't a mystery, where the clues had to piece together to make a perfect picture. But how had Monique's stalker left the message? And could Kenzie's tormentor figure out a way to do the same? Were her abductors already in Kansas? Or even on this same flight?

Cole set the book aside, excused himself and pushed his way to the aisle. Walking slowly toward the bathroom, he let his gaze roam, looking for a familiar face, a leather jacket, something that would make this feel like the bus ride all over again.

No one set off any alarm bells. He stepped into the bathroom and stood, staring at himself in the mirror, trying not to allow the question to form in his mind. But it was already there. Already screaming at him.

What if he was too late?

The Jacobs's farmhouse sat back from the road, its two-story frame covered with white siding. Faded green shutters and wide concrete steps should have made it appear worn but instead gave the place a casual, down-home look.

Except, even with a car parked in the driveway, it didn't look like anyone was home. No porch lights sent a welcoming beam into the growing darkness. No light spilled from the living room window or around the edges of the curtains in the bedrooms.

No light at all.

Cole blinked as that sank in, but he pushed back the sudden panic. Kenzie could be out with her mom, or in a back room where the light wouldn't show from here.

Or her abductors could have beaten him there, after all.

Taking a deep breath, Cole parked his rental car. There was nowhere to hide it—just a lawn full of green grass, a lone tree and a long, cracked sidewalk. He trotted to the steps and took them two at a time. When no one answered his knock, he opened his phone. He'd try Kenzie, then Mrs. Jacobs. She wouldn't answer the cell, but if he heard it ring inside, and no one answered the home phone…Cole dialed. He lowered his phone, listening for the ring. Nothing. The land line ring was shrill enough to be heard outside, but still no answer.

He was too late.

Again.

Breathing in loud, rapid gasps, Cole remembered flashing blue lights. An open ambulance door. The firemen and paramedics working to pull Allison from the wreckage. He'd been on his way home, trying to call her to find out why she hadn't shown and when they could arrange a talk. But she hadn't answered, and even amid the chaos, he'd heard the personalized ring tone she'd given him.

Cole leaned against the house, feeling the guilt close in. It had suffocated him then and was threatening to now. Kenzie—

Someone died for me once.

He heard her voice, saw the sorrow and earnestness on her face as she'd tried to reach him. He'd saved her life once. She'd saved his forever by showing him what it felt like to love someone enough to be willing to die for them. Even when they turned away.

Cole was guilty, but he was forgiven. It was time to leave the past behind and take care of the present. Which meant searching every inch of this property if he had to in order to find MacKenzie Jacobs.

Taking a steadying breath, he tried the knob. Unlocked.

After picking at a piece of cheesecake, Kenzie finally excused herself from Needa and Frank's house. If Needa did as promised, she'd be faking an injury any moment now in order to convince Eleanor to spend the night. Even though it was probably too late to avoid bringing trouble here, Kenzie wanted her mother out of the line of fire.

She slipped out the door and made a beeline for her mother's house, trying to think about anything but the darkness. Half an acre of clear land lit by a sliver of the moon. Nothing to worry about. She'd just keep her head down, walk fast, and—

An unfamiliar car was parked in the driveway. Kenzie shivered, halting near the edge of Needa's home. The moonlight cast enough of a glow for her to tell that no one sat in the other vehicle.

Mom hadn't been expecting anyone. At least, she hadn't mentioned it before heading next door. Kenzie studied the lawn. Still didn't see anyone. If this was a movie, the scary music would be playing about now. The women in the theater would be squeezing the hands of their men, whispering warnings for the heroine: Don't go inside. Don't be a fool.

She never watched those kinds of movies, and, as her muscles quivered to the point she could hardly walk the rest of the way, she knew why. She didn't have the guts. No inner strength here. All the good stuff went to Mikey.

And he was dead.

Half crouching, she forced herself to move. When she reached her mother's car, she slipped inside and opened the glove compartment, shielding the light as well as she could. A heavy flashlight filled her hand, as expected. Eleanor Jacobs was nothing if not predictable. She pulled it free, hefted it, didn't snap it on. Maybe it wasn't an ideal weapon, but it'd do a better job than her cold curling iron.

She glided out of the car, bracing her rubbery limbs against it. What was she doing besides getting herself killed?

Maybe this could end. Right here, right now, in the same place Mikey died.

The front door was half-open. If someone was in there, with all the shadows and crooks and crannies and memories—

The door swung open the rest of the way and a long shadow stepped onto the porch. A man, holding something. She inched closer, keeping low between the vehicles.

He turned, his back half toward her. She raced the rest of the way as he reached for the knob. Pulled it closed.

She slammed the flashlight against his head.

Whirling, Cole threw the flowers he'd brought at his attacker's face. He leaped to the side, crouched, then froze.

"Cole?" Kenzie stared at him, her eyes luminous in the moonlight, rose petals settling around her feet. Alive. Safe. And ready to clobber him again.

"You're okay. Thank God." A warm rush of relief filled him, and he barely restrained himself from wrapping her in a tight hug.

"What are you doing here? Did you just hit me with… flowers?"

He grinned, nearly giddy with the sight of her. "Hey, you're the one who clubbed me." The grin turned to a grimace as he felt the spot. It was tender and slightly moist. Bleeding.

She reached inside and flipped on the porch light. "I'm sorry." Her voice was soft but tinged with hysteria. "But what are you doing here? Sneaking around, breaking in, nearly giving me a heart attack—"

"When what I really wanted to do was give you roses— an even dozen to make up for the last bouquet you received." Still holding his head, Cole backed away from the door, giving her space. This probably wasn't the best way to show her he was on her side. But then, she'd scared him first. His heart still beat triple time. "I got worried when I didn't see any lights. Then nobody answered either phone."

Her face held a mixture of relief and incredulity. "You flew to Kansas because I didn't return a call?"

So she did think he was a stalker. He sighed. All he wanted was for her to be safe. Maybe he'd misunderstood her intentions—her trip hadn't been about rejecting his protection in order to keep him safe. It was just about rejecting him, period.

"I'm sorry I scared you. I was worried." Cole backed up another step. One more and he'd go over the edge.

No. He'd done that already.

"I just went next door with my mom." Kenzie glanced down at the ruined bouquet, then back at him.

Cole noticed the goose bumps on her arms when she moved closer. Without thinking, he slid his hands down her forearms, trying to warm them. "Are you okay, Zee?" he asked softly, bending down to look her straight in the eye.

"Yes," she whispered, her gaze shifting to his mouth.

He fingered a strand of her hair—so silky—then, his heart thudding hard against his rib cage, he cupped his hand behind her neck. She tilted her head, and he leaned in, kissing her gently, tasting the sweetness of her lips. Her hands met behind his head, her fingers entangled in his hair, and he deepened the kiss, felt her mouth move against his—

She jerked back, eyes wide. "Cole…" Her voice was breathless, urgent. "You shouldn't be here, Cole."

It took a moment for the true meaning of that to sink in. Oh, she was good at whittling, all right. She'd carefully chipped away the walls of his heart, then thrust her knife deep inside.

Cole waited until he could breathe, then turned and walked away, bleeding from more than the cut on his head.

* * *

It wasn't until Cole slid into the driver's seat that Kenzie's words came back to her, and by then it was too late. He spun out of the drive before she could stop him. Standing at the edge of the yard, she watched his taillights fade into the distance. The sudden ache in her heart must be a faint echo of his own. *"You shouldn't be here, Cole…"*

"I didn't mean it that way," she whispered into the darkness. It wasn't that she didn't trust him, that she thought he had not-so-upright intentions—she'd seen the brokenness in his face when he'd confessed his past sins. And that's what they were—past. Forgiven. Forgotten.

She touched her lips, still tingling from his warmth as the black of the night settled over her. She turned to face the house, the porch light beckoning. Kenzie half jogged to the front door, then locked it securely behind her and headed to the back to do the same there, flipping light switches in each room she passed. The door in the kitchen was already locked…but no dead bolt. She shoved a chair under the doorknob, then pushed the table up against it.

Now to check the windows. She paused in the living room, staring out into the lonely night. Cole might be gone forever. The thought hollowed out her insides. That alone told her pushing him away was the best thing she could do.

The glass chilled her fingers as she stretched her hand against the window. *Good-bye, Cole.* She tapped the glass once and pulled away.

The house was deathly silent except for the ticking of the grandfather clock, so much like the phone calls. *Tick-tock. Tick-tock.* A steady, foreboding rhythm, standing witness as the seconds, minutes, hours passed by. Waiting to sound the death knell.

She checked the lock and closed the curtain. Mom was

tucked away at the neighbors' house. Cole was surely on his way back to Atlanta. Or maybe even Texas. Detective Parker was tracking leads, or maybe even working another case. Right now, it was just her and the stalker—out there somewhere, preparing for the next round.

What a comforting thought right before bedtime.

Kenzie checked the last window, switched on one more light and retreated to her room. Even with the blinds closed and curtains drawn, her skin crawled as she changed into her pajamas. No one could be watching, and yet…

She was becoming paranoid. At this rate, she'd attack the grandfather clock when it chimed the hour.

Stop it.

The sheets smelled musty. Kenzie checked them—clean— then crawled under the blanket. Her nerves zinged; she felt ready to jump at the slightest noise. She was almost afraid to close her eyes, afraid to see which face would haunt her during the midnight hours. Mikey? Or Cole, standing at the end of a long hall, wearing an expression of confused pain.

No sleeping tonight. She placed her laptop on the bed beside her. And bit back a scream.

An open document displayed a message, spelled out in bold type: *You can run but you cannot hide.*

TWENTY

Cole went through the McDonald's drive-through, then parked the car and nursed a cup of coffee. He should be back with Kenzie, apologizing for walking away, convincing her that all he wanted to do was help, assuring her that he was a new person now, partly thanks to that sermonette she'd preached at him.

They should be sitting in the kitchen—the table safely between them—talking out theories and ideas, waking up Parker to see if he'd tracked down the YouTube guy yet. And when Kenzie got too tired to keep her eyes open, he'd make coffee and stay awake while she slept.

Instead, he was doing the coffee thing miles away, where it did her no good. Yeah, she'd hurt him, but that didn't matter. He'd deserved it. He had two choices: get a flight to Texas and forget about everything, or go back to Atlanta with Kenzie and see it through to the end.

Cole pictured Kenzie—alone in a place haunted by memories of her brother's death, the house lit up to ward away fear but not quite accomplishing that feat—and his hand hit the gearshift. He shouldn't have left her alone this long.

When he reached her street, he drove past the homestead and found a place near a house across the street—far enough away that she might not notice his car, but close enough that he could watch to see anyone approaching her house. The darkness hid a lot, but with the wide open spaces, any glint of light should be easily spotted.

Sipping his coffee, Cole studied the farmhouse. The blinds were closed, but the edges were illuminated. With bright rooms and no storms, Kenzie should have her fear in check. Maybe she'd sleep after all.

With his seat slightly tilted back, Cole shifted until he found a relatively comfortable position and raised his coffee once more, ready for a long night.

A siren blared. Cole straightened to find red-and-blue lights coming toward him.

Toward Kenzie.

There'd been no other signs of an intruder. Nothing missing or damaged. The only things out of order were the pieces of furniture she'd used to secure the doors. Kenzie gave the policeman her report with a trembling voice while her mother glared at the room in general. A confrontation was coming, but Kenzie didn't care. All that mattered was that someone had violated her sense of security once again.

And she was terrified that it might have been Cole.

What other explanation could there be? He'd had the opportunity. He'd been around just about every time something had happened.

But she couldn't believe it. Not now. Not after he'd told her his darkest secret. Not after he'd kissed her like he loved her. Like she was a treasure.

Right now, though, she felt like an animal. Hunted, cornered, teased and taunted. But not by Cole. Not him.

The policeman asked her a question but was interrupted as his partner barged through the door. Panting, slightly disheveled and hauling a man in handcuffs.

Cole.

His eyes, wild with worry, settled when they landed on her. He stared at her as if he were drinking her in, trying to convince himself that she was okay. Well, she wasn't. And she was afraid she never would be again.

Being slammed in the head twice in one night hadn't been on Cole's agenda. Making Kenzie cry hadn't, either. But the tears had started as soon as she had laid eyes on him, and when the cop jerked him to the side of the kitchen, Kenzie cried harder.

His relief at seeing her unhurt mingled with his confusion. What in tarnation had he done this time?

Mrs. Jacobs studied Kenzie with an expression of…shock, maybe? She awkwardly patted her daughter's arm, then glared at Cole. "What did you do to my daughter?"

Good question.

"He didn't do anything." Kenzie stepped forward, dashing her tears away with the back of her hand. Before the cops could stop her, she was in Cole's face.

To do what? Hit him again? His head throbbed already. What was a little more?

She grabbed a napkin off the table and pulled his head down. The cut stung as she dabbed at it, but her touch soothed everything else.

"I'm so sorry, Cole," she whispered. Her breath warmed his ear, and something hot splashed on his neck. She must still be crying. "I didn't know they would— What are you doing here? Again?"

"Same as before." A wry smile crossed his lips. "Protecting you."

Laughter burst from her. Hearing it—slightly hysterical, but genuine—made being tackled by a two-hundred-plus-pound officer of the law almost worth it.

"I found him running toward the house," that same officer stated.

"And that was good enough cause to handcuff him?" Kenzie asked.

"He resisted."

Cole rolled his eyes.

"Well, let him go, okay? It was a misunderstanding. Sorry for wasting your time."

Cole squinted, trying to read her expression around the pounding headache. What had happened? Why had she called the police?

The cop with the notebook flipped it closed. "You sure, Miss Jacobs?"

"Yes. All a misunderstanding." Kenzie cut off whatever her mother was about to say. "Cole's a friend." Her gaze caught his and held. "We're good here." She waited until his hands were free, then herded the officers toward the door. "Thank you so much."

They made their exit, and Mrs. Jacobs folded her arms to glower at both of them this time. "Kenzie, you have a lot of explaining to do. You, too, Mr. Leighton."

"Yes, ma'am." Cole stayed near the entrance, but eased the door closed behind him. No more ambushes tonight, unless this stern woman in front of him intended to do it.

"While Kenzie grabs the first aid kit—under the kitchen sink, dear—you need to tell me exactly why I shouldn't call the police back to haul you away."

Cole swallowed hard, meeting Kenzie's eyes as she reentered the room with a small white box. "Because I care very much for your daughter, and I would do anything to keep her safe."

As she stared at him, her ultrablue eyes red-rimmed and tired, he bit his lip. This wasn't the way he'd wanted to tell her, with him utterly exhausted and her traumatized by… whatever had happened since he'd left the house. Blood dripped from his cut, making his eye twitch. He even had a coffee stain on his shirt. But there it was—though he'd known her less than two weeks, he cared. So much that it brought a silly grin to his face.

Which her mother immediately removed with one question: "What if she doesn't want you here?"

What if she didn't? What if, instead of helping, he was actually holding up progress? Somehow he kept pulling the focus of the investigation onto himself. He was slowing things down, complicating things by his very presence. He should go back to Texas, and…and leave Kenzie's protection in the hands of a competent but skeptical detective who didn't know about her intense fear of storms and darkness. Okay, so that wouldn't stop Parker from solving the case, but the man probably had a family. If the choice came to sacrifice himself so that Kenzie could live, Parker might hesitate a brief moment, because the detective didn't love her.

Kenzie watched as something changed on Cole's face. His scrutiny of her intensified while his eyes grew incredibly soft. He didn't answer her mother's question; he didn't have to. If she turned him away, Cole would respect her wishes and leave the house, but he'd park right across the street in case she needed him.

"I want him here." Heat rose to her face, but she didn't look away. Instead, she leaned closer under the pretense of attending to his injury.

Cole smiled, his eyes crinkling at the corners, then his face sobered. "What happened, Zee?"

She'd managed to forget the message while drowning in his gaze. Now the fear came crashing back down. She pointed to the laptop she'd left on the table. "Someone typed a note on my computer while I was out tonight. I found it after you left."

He flinched and searched her face, probably looking for signs that she suspected him. Firmly, she held his gaze for a moment before retreating to pick out the correct size bandage.

After drawing a breath, he quoted it word for word.

Kenzie's stomach flip-flopped, but again she stared him in the face. "It was in *Obsession*?"

Cole nodded and opened his mouth, but her mother broke in, reminding them of her presence. "That's the book you modeled for, right?"

That cursed cover. Kenzie managed a nod.

"MacKenzie Ann, you tell me what's going on. Right. Now." She thumped her hand against the table and folded her arms.

Kenzie shook her head. "It's nothing you need to worry about, Mom. It's being handled back home, then I'll be out of your hair soon." Her words came out harsh, and they both stared at her, eyebrows raised.

Cole must have sensed the rising tension. "I think I'll let you two get caught up. Is there somewhere I could— I mean, would you mind if…?"

His awkward attempt to invite himself to spend the night gave Kenzie a brief reprieve as Eleanor Jacobs filled her hostess role. Cole stepped outside to grab his bag from the car, and the room felt a little colder with him gone, the air a little harder to breathe.

Then Cole retreated to Mikey's old room, and she and her mother moved to Kenzie's room to face off. If this confrontation had to happen, she was going to do it in the comfort of the bedroom.

"I want to hear it all, MacKenzie. Don't gloss anything over, and don't shrug me off. I won't take it anymore."

Kenzie blinked. Where was the indifferent mother she'd had all her life?

When she'd finished telling the crazy story, Mom stewed it over in silence, lounging beside her on the bed. Kenzie waited. Would she laugh it off? Say her daughter had finally gone off the deep end, was truly paranoid? Or would she lay the blame on Cole, who slept below them?

He cared about her. He was willingly putting himself in danger, refusing to go away. What did she do with that? She was too exhausted to think about it.

Her mother finally broke the strained silence. "Why didn't you tell me, MacKenzie?"

"I…didn't want to worry you. There was really nothing you could do."

"You didn't want to bother me, you mean."

Kenzie didn't answer. After a moment, Mom slammed a fist into the pillow, shaking the bed. Kenzie blinked, glanced down, then returned her stare to the ceiling.

"Why not? I'm your mother, but you allowed me to believe it was all over. I might not have been able to catch any criminals, but I could have prayed for you, been there when you were scared."

This time, Kenzie lowered her gaze. "Why? You've never wanted to do that before." She hadn't meant to say it—had hardly even thought it before the words had popped out.

Wide-eyed, with quivering lips, Mom turned her head but did not speak.

"I mean, I had nightmares after Mikey died, and I don't remember you ever being there. I know you lost your favorite child, and I know it was my fault, but did you even—" Kenzie cut off as her mother pounded the pillow again.

"You listen to me." Her voice shook as she sat up straight. "I loved you both, and I love you still. I related to Mikey better—

I was raised with all boys, without a mother. Then, after Mikey, you were so independent. His death wasn't your fault, but you wouldn't believe otherwise. The guilt I felt—we should have been here that night, your father and I. Should have been here—"

Mom sobbed, interrupting the flow of words, but she held up a hand, silently commanding Kenzie to let her finish. "After he died, you withdrew. I couldn't comfort you—you wouldn't let me. I never knew about the nightmares, MacKenzie. I would have tried to be there. But then…then I didn't know how to reach you anymore. And, it was wrong, but I quit trying."

A lump burned in Kenzie's throat as her mother choked back another sob.

"It's not that I don't love you. It's that you don't let me, because you don't let me *in*."

The blood drained from Kenzie's face—from her entire body, it felt. Bleeding out on the bed without a single visible wound. Her mother wanted to love her—had tried to—and she hadn't allowed it? Is that what she was doing to Cole—the real reason she'd run away from him, why she hadn't told him she cared for him, too, when she knew deep down that she did?

Is that what she was doing with God? He wanted to show her His love, but was she holding herself back because of fear?

"You don't let me in."

Her heart cried out in anguish. God's words of assurance had been there all along, hadn't they? She'd wanted someone to know her well, to care about the little things. He knew how many hairs were on her head. How was that for detailed knowledge and care?

I'm sorry, God. So sorry. I love You. I know You love me, too. Help me to let down the walls I've built around my heart.

This time as Kenzie cried herself to sleep, her mother wrapped her in a comforting embrace.

TWENTY-ONE

As pink fingers of dawn began to light up the darkness, Cole felt his way down the hall. Between listening for intruders and trying to come up with a plan to end Kenzie's torment, he'd hardly slept.

Apparently Kenzie hadn't fared any better. The kitchen light was already on, and she sat in the breakfast nook, hugging her knees to her chest.

"Morning, Kenzie," Cole said softly. "Want me to make some coffee?" What would it be like to have this as a morning routine? To have her part of his life, always?

"Just push the button. It's ready to go."

As the scent of fresh brewed coffee filled the room, Cole settled on the bench across from her. "Couldn't sleep?"

"I did some."

She met his eyes with her shadowed ones, and he reached over to squeeze her hands. They were cold.

"What am I going to do, Cole?" Her voice trembled slightly.

"First, we're going to have some coffee. Then it's time for a strategy session. We'll figure it out, Kenzie."

"But…what if they come back? Someone put that message on my computer." She glanced toward her laptop on the table between them.

"They won't." He hoped he was right. "It's not in the book." He got up to pour the coffee and retrieve his notes, then returned to his seat. "So everything has happened—molded to fit your life, of course—up to about three-fourths of the way through the book, right?"

"I think so." Kenzie hadn't touched her mug, and her legs were still pressed tightly against her. "The next thing that happens to Monique is the second abduction."

"Right." Cole studied her carefully. "You okay? You're shivering."

"Fine. Let's just get this over with."

He held her gaze. "You won't face this alone."

"I know." She finally gave him a small smile.

He returned to his notes. "So it happens while Monique is in a store parking lot, going to her car. And we're pretty sure, from what the YouTube guy said, that they're going to try for tomorrow. Monday."

"How would they know I was going to a store? I mean, what if I just stayed home all day? What then?"

"Do you have any habits—any set times you go somewhere on Mondays?"

She shuddered again, and Cole felt the chill pass through his own body. How long had they been watching her? Would she ever feel truly safe again?

"Zee." He waited until she looked at him. "Come here." He patted the seat beside him.

It took a moment, but she finally placed her feet on the floor and walked to the other side of the table. She sat beside him, back rigid. He allowed himself to smile at her, but nothing more. No pushing. He was there if she needed him.

She kept silent, fidgeting. Missing her knife and blocks of wood? "I work out on Mondays," she finally said. "At a gym in a shopping plaza." A shiver shook her, and she inched closer until her shoulder skimmed his arm. "That would be close enough to the book scenario, right?"

"I think so."

"So you think that's where they'll try to hit. The parking lot after one of my normal workouts."

She'd probably be tired, her hands filled with a gym bag and water bottle. If a van sped up to her and she wasn't expecting it, there'd be little time to react. They could slide open the side door, grab her, drag her inside.

But now they'd lost the element of surprise. "We can talk to Parker and set a trap—have you go in the building, but a double comes out. If they have enough undercover people in the area…"

Kenzie sighed and leaned her cheek against his shoulder. "Just fly home, hang out until tomorrow, then go to the gym and the nightmare will be over?"

Her damp hair smelled fresh and clean. Cole rested his chin against her head. "I hope so." There was nothing he wanted more than to see Kenzie safe. Yet, when this threat was over…would their relationship be, too?

"And if the trap doesn't work?"

"It'll work." It had to. "I'll call Parker now." He pulled out his cell phone, but Kenzie curled a hand around his arm, tugging it back down, twining her fingers with his.

"Not yet."

Cole slowly settled the phone onto the table as Kenzie tucked her feet up on the bench and buried her head in his chest. He willed his heartbeat not to speed up. It didn't obey.

When her breathing slowed and steadied, he dared to lean down far enough to catch a glimpse of her face. The anxiety had eased out of her expression, leaving her to peaceful sleep. The ache in his heart intensified. He wanted to hold her forever, keep her safe, just like this.

But there were things that needed to be done first. Her laptop still rested on the table. Cole hesitated, then carefully pulled it toward him and switched it on. He wanted to see the note for himself, and he needed to buy their airline tickets.

A desert background lit the screen, then icons appeared neatly lined up on the side. As it finished loading, Eleanor Jacobs walked into the room and smiled wearily as she met his eyes over Kenzie's head.

Cole smiled back, suddenly conscious of his scruffy appearance—wrinkled clothing, unshaved face, tousled hair. Not the best look to win over her mother. Of course, he hadn't quite won over Kenzie yet, had he?

Cole turned his attention to the screen, nodding his thanks when Eleanor refilled his mug. Only a few seats were left on the flight he'd chosen, and the other flights departing today were filled. Trying not to wake Kenzie, he pulled out his credit card and paid for their tickets. He minimized the itinerary, took a sip of coffee and put his hand back on the touch pad.

Nothing happened. The screen blinked—once, twice. A box appeared in the upper right corner. And then the cursor moved, sliding across the screen of its own accord.

As Cole narrowed his eyes, the flight itinerary filled the screen once more. He ran a finger over the touch pad again. The cursor moved as he directed, then jerked back to where it had started, scrolling down the entire page before minimizing it once again.

"Mrs. Jacobs," he said softly. "Did Kenzie say anything about her computer acting up?"

Kenzie grunted and shifted her position slightly before whispering, "It's fine, as far as I know."

He tried to keep his voice calm. "Watch."

She opened her eyes as a new document opened up. And then the computer began to type. By itself.

Kenzie pulled away, rising to her feet, pointing at the laptop. Cole felt like doing the same, or maybe heaving the offending computer out the window as he stared at the screen, watching words form.

Time is running out. Tick. Tock.

"What's going on?" Eleanor asked in a pinched voice.

Cole watched as the cursor blinked and no other letters appeared. Then the arrow moved to the box, the screen flickered and he was in control once again.

"I don't know exactly what happened, but it looks like you didn't have an intruder after all." When they planted the bugs in Kenzie's house, they must have put some sort of remote access program on her computer, too. The relief that flooded through him at that thought was short-lived. "But whoever it is has access to all of Kenzie's files. And…" He avoided Kenzie's eyes. "Now he knows our flight schedule."

"Leighton." Parker's gruff voice grated Cole's ears as he checked his voice mail. "I've been calling for the past hour. Where are you?" End of message.

Such a polite guy. A half smile twisted the corner of Cole's mouth as he led the way toward baggage claim. Kenzie walked half a step behind him, her fingers laced through his.

"Who was that?"

"Parker. He must have some news. Sounds impatient." A new lead? A confirmation of the plan they'd come up with? He should call now, but he would wait until they weren't on the move. Right now, he wanted every sense alert to danger.

The farther they walked, the tighter and colder Kenzie's grip became. They'd taken the walkway instead of the tram— fewer people—but the echo of their footsteps on tile put his nerves on edge.

As they stepped off the escalator, he kept an eye out for

anyone suspicious, but without much of a description past what the gunmen had been wearing a week ago, that was hard to do. Half the people milling around them could be the enemy. Cole quick-stepped to the baggage claim, found the right carousel and pulled Kenzie closer, positioning her near a wall with his body blocking access to her as they waited. Then he punched Parker's number into his phone.

"Leighton, it's about time."

"Sorry, sir. We just got off the plane."

"You're with Miss Jacobs?"

Cole frowned. "Yes."

"Is someone picking you up?"

"No. I'm renting another car. What's going on?"

A heavy sigh. "Not sure. You know that book of yours?"

"Not mine, sir. Warren Flint's."

"Yeah. That one. Does it say anything about murder?"

Cole stepped closer to Kenzie, trying to stay calm as his eyes swept the crowd once again. "No."

"That's what I thought. We finally tracked down the man who posted the video online—took a while getting through red tape to get his IP address. Anyway, he's dead, as of this morning, looks like. We confiscated his computer, but it's been wiped clean. Apparently our guy didn't appreciate his crime being displayed on the World Wide Web."

Which one had been accessing Kenzie's computer? "No possibility it's unrelated?"

"I highly doubt it."

So did Cole.

"Maybe this means he'll stick with the book and just pick up a new partner, or maybe go solo. But if he doesn't…"

"The plan is off?"

"At this point I'm saying we go through with it. I'm making preparations. But Miss Jacobs needs to be extra careful. I'm working on getting some protection for her, but we have some other big cases going down, so we're running short."

Even though Kenzie could not hear, fear darkened her eyes. But she met his gaze, blinked and nodded. She was still with him.

"I'll stay with her."

"Good." The sound muffled for a moment, then Parker came back on. "I gotta go, but, Leigh   careful. I've got a bad feeling."

"What's going on?" Kenzie asked as he slid the phone onto its clip.

"I'll tell you in the car." Their luggage had circled at least once, but he hadn't wanted to leave her side. He spotted her bag with his nearby and pulled her closer to the carousel. "Let's grab the bags and get out of here."

"Cole, you're scaring me."

He shot her what he hoped was a reassuring smile. "I'm scaring myself. Come on." He hoisted his suitcase and scanned the area while Kenzie tugged hers free. He should have called John to pick them up. His cousin's broad shoulders and tough-guy looks would offer more protection. Someone to watch Kenzie's back while Cole cleared a path to the door. Instead, they were on their own.

Not true. God was with them, and this time Cole actually believed it. *Protect Kenzie, Jesus. Watch over her. You make a much better hero than I.*

Clutching her bag in one hand and Cole's arm with the other, Kenzie hurried toward the rental cars. She felt like a doe during hunting season, darting around trees and through thick foliage, trying to escape an unknown enemy. But it might be Cole that got caught in the crosshairs. He claimed he wanted to be here—would be, whether she liked it or not. And she did like it. His presence calmed her. Made her feel…beloved.

But Kenzie wanted him out of danger. If anything happened to him…

Cole suddenly jerked her closer, his eyes roaming the area. "What's wrong, Zee?"

Her heart skipped a beat, then calmed. "Nothing. I'm sorry. I was just thinking." He sensed too much. Would she never be able to hide anything from him?

Relaxing his grip, his gaze raked her face. "Tell me."

She broke eye contact. "About the book. The part where Monique changes her appearance. She was ready to walk away from everything in order to…" Save the people she loved. Kenzie groaned inwardly. She wasn't strong enough to face her enemies alone. Paralyzed by fear, as always. *God, what do I have to do to become strong? To stand tall and fearless, trusting You to take care of me…and my loved ones?*

"And?" Cole gently tipped her chin up.

Kenzie stared at his chest, a guitar emblazoned on his shirt. "I'm not Monique. I'm not as brave as she was."

His hand moved to the back of her head, fingers tangled in her hair, and he leaned down until his forehead rested against hers. "No, you're not Monique. You're determined to go back and face it, to do whatever you have to do to find justice. That sounds pretty brave to me."

Cole raised his head to scan their surroundings, pushing her face against his chest. She settled her arms around his waist and soaked in his warmth. Just for one moment, then it was time to go.

In the car, the warmth slipped away as Cole told her what

Detective Parker had said. The book was creepy, but it worked as a guide. If the man with the island accent decided to ditch the playbook, he could be anywhere. Do anything. And he might not wait until Monday.

TWENTY-TWO

After watching the Chevy's rearview mirror through a series of odd twists and turns that almost got him lost, Cole parked in the lot next to John's apartment building. He'd picked a different kind of car this time—a white Cobalt. If the murderer had put Cole on his watch list, maybe the new vehicle would earn them a surveillance-free day or two.

He rushed Kenzie inside, wavering between fear of someone leaping from between the cars and the feeling that he was a bad actor sneaking around the set of a low-budget suspense flick. Give him dark shades and a trench coat and he'd be good to go.

Once inside, though, the building was familiar territory. He punched the button for the elevator, angling his body to watch the exit. The doors dinged open. Empty. Kenzie hit the Five for John's floor, and a perky pop song filled the elevator. It felt off—a *Jaws* soundtrack should be playing instead. The shark was out there, circling, playing games with their heads.

Kenzie stood beside him—still, quiet and pale. She probably shouldn't stay at John's, but until they figured out a better place, this would have to do. Should they camp out at the police station? For once, it didn't sound like Parker wanted to lock him up. Maybe because Cole had been in Kansas when the murder had taken place. Or maybe the detective had decided to trust the results of the lie detector test after all.

The elevator glided to a stop, settled, then opened to the hallway. Again, empty. A relieved sigh escaped Kenzie, and he squeezed her hand. Five doors down, and they'd be there— safe for the moment in the familiar environment where Mikey's knife waited to be reclaimed.

"Almost there." He smiled down at Kenzie. Put some wood in her hand and the color might come back to her face.

At John's door, Cole fitted a key into the lock. He pushed it open, waved Kenzie past him and set their luggage against the inside wall. Turned to lock the door just in time to see the last of the blood drain from Kenzie's face.

Before he could say a word, Kenzie's palm smacked over his mouth. She drew a finger to her lips, eyes wide and desperately afraid. Had she seen something? Heard someone? Nothing appeared to be amiss. Cole moved until his body shielded hers, listening intently. A faint voice came from John's room. A rhythmic flow—no music. He stepped closer, straining to hear, but Kenzie jerked him back.

The stark terror on her face propelled him out the door. He closed it, then turned to her. "What's wrong? What did you see?"

"You didn't hear him?" she hissed through chattering teeth. "Didn't recognize his voice?"

Cole shook his head, keeping his hand on the doorknob to make sure it didn't swing open.

"*He's* in there. Talking to your cousin."

"Slow down, Zee. I'm not with you." Or maybe he was and just didn't want to believe it. "Are you saying your abductor is in the apartment with John?"

"I heard him, Cole." Hysteria tinged her tone. "I couldn't make out the words, but that's his voice. It's him."

"Okay." Cole pressed a hand against her shoulder. "Then this will end sooner than we'd planned, right?"

Kenzie swallowed. Nodded. Panted a couple breaths and nodded again. "What do I need to do?"

"Go to the car." He handed over the keys, forcing her fingers to curl around them when she tried to protest. "Call Parker. Hide. Pray. Keep your cell phone on."

"But—"

"Do it, Zee."

She bit her lip, hesitated for an eternity and raced back down the hall.

Kenzie hit the bottom floor, watched the doors open, but couldn't bring herself to step out. The detective answered on the first ring. As she filled him in, she stayed in the elevator, staring across the empty lobby, holding the door open until their conversation ended. She should obey Cole. In her head she understood. Stay out of the way so he didn't have to concentrate on protecting her as well as himself. With her tucked away somewhere safe, she couldn't be used as the gunman's bargaining chip again.

But what if Cole needed help? A quick diversion to give him the upper hand? Or what if Cole was about to become that bargaining chip? If anything happened to him because of her…

No. Cole wasn't going to be another Mikey. He wasn't going to try to fix her problems while she hid out, waiting in safety.

Snapping the phone closed, Kenzie pressed the Five again. The elevator lifted. Her stomach lurched. She closed her eyes and breathed in…out…in again. Trying not to think about what she might find in the apartment. *God, keep Cole safe.*

The hallway was deathly still, like the calm after the rush

of a tornado. Kenzie closed the distance to where the apartment door stood slightly ajar, and she glided to the other side. Through the crack, everything appeared normal. No furniture overturned or blood splattered.

But in the background—soft, yet distinct with its lilting ebb and flow—came the voice.

She scooted into the kitchen, picked up a bar stool and stepped closer to the back room. Hoisting her makeshift weapon, she charged down the hallway and burst into the bedroom.

Cole and John swung to face her.

The voice said, "Hello, sweetheart. I told you we'd meet again."

TWENTY-THREE

Cole grabbed Kenzie before she could swing the stool, but he would have allowed her to hit him if that would take that bloodless, horrified expression off her face.

"Kenzie! It's okay!" John carefully extracted the stool from her grip, and Cole wrapped her trembling body in a bear hug. "Cut the sound, John."

The voice ceased, leaving only the rasping of his breath and Kenzie's gulping half sobs as she tried to wrench free.

Cole held on. "He's not here, Kenzie. Listen to me: It's a recording. Nothing more."

When she stopped struggling, Cole loosened his grip. Her eyes were still wild, but she wasn't going to faint...or tear John apart with her bare hands.

"John was listening to an audiobook. That's the voice we heard. No one else is here." But Parker would be in just a few minutes. Maybe by then his heart rate would be back to normal.

Kenzie stilled, staring toward the stereo system.

"I'm sorry I scared you, Kenzie," John said, his tone helping to soothe even Cole's frayed nerves. John was okay. They were all okay.

And they might have stumbled across the key to the case.

Cole laid an arm around her shoulder, tucking her close. Still trembling. It must be the right guy, but just in case… "Do you want to hear it again? Make sure that's the voice?"

She nodded, but her eyes held no doubt. John started the recording and handed the CD case to Kenzie as the story once again filled the room.

> *"Monique stared into the face of the man who'd haunted her nightmares. This time, no ski mask hid him from her. In the waning light, she traced his features— wide-set eyes, slightly hooked nose, thin lips, pasty- white skin. Unattractive in a forgettable way. But she would not forget."*

"Enough," Kenzie said.

John instantly stopped the CD and turned to her. "I wanted to listen to the story, see if there was anything I could do to help this end."

Kenzie didn't seem to hear him. Her thumb rubbed hard against the title, spelled out in a large, bold font. *Obsession.*

Cole took her fingers in his and held them as he studied the plastic case along with her. On the back, two men smiled up at them: Warren Flint, the author; and Luther Tillette, the voice artist. Tillette didn't wear a ski mask, and he didn't have pasty skin or a hooked nose. He was handsome enough, with a suave smile, a golden-brown face…

And a brown leather jacket.

Something slammed against the outside door. As John moved to run interference, Cole shoved Kenzie out of sight and planted himself close by. No one was getting to Kenzie except over his dead body.

"Police department! Come out and show yourself!"

Two uniformed officers came into view, guns ready. Cole eased Kenzie back up but didn't allow her to move into the open until he heard Parker barking commands.

"False alarm," Cole said as he walked into the kitchen.

Parker didn't lower his gun until Kenzie stepped behind Cole. "Everything okay, Miss Jacobs?"

She nodded, and Cole moved aside, studying her as the police checked the rest of the apartment. The fear had mostly drained from her features. In its place was rock-hard determination.

"What happened?" the detective asked.

Cole opened his mouth, but Kenzie spoke first.

"I was wrong about the island accent."

Parker narrowed his gaze. Cole felt himself doing the same.

Kenzie stared at the case of the audiobook. "He's from Belize."

Luther Tillette. Failed actor turned successful voice artist. Aspiring screenwriter, apparently—one who took his creativity too seriously. Either that, or one who had turned this project into an obsession. Creative license didn't mean he had a license to kill. Or to kidnap or stalk or anything else.

Cole glared at the face on his computer screen. Tillette lived in New Jersey. How he'd found Kenzie in Atlanta was anyone's guess, although when Cole had called Flint, the author had said he'd mentioned the city as well as Kenzie's occupation in a few interviews.

He tipped back the chair and looked into John's living room. Kenzie was curled into a tight ball on the sofa, arms draped protectively around herself even in fitful sleep. She should be at a hotel somewhere—comfortable and under the careful watch of hired bodyguards. But she wanted to be here, with him and John, because she couldn't bring herself to trust anyone else.

She trusted him. With that heavy responsibility came joy. A sweet, beautiful, courageous woman believed in him, even knowing his sins. MacKenzie Jacobs, with her deep fears and deeper capacity for love, made him want to be a better man.

No, she'd *already* made him a better man. He was still aware of his unworthiness. But now he saw it from a different angle. The sin of his past. The purifying touch of grace. The hope of the future.

Kenzie had helped him to understand Jesus a little more.

I'm not turning my back on Your love anymore, Jesus. Thank You for Your sacrifice. Thank You for a second chance.

John sauntered out of the kitchen over to the computer desk. "They catch him yet?" he asked softly as he read Cole's notes.

"Parker hasn't called."

"So we wait."

Cole nodded and picked up his mug. The coffee was lukewarm and bitter, but he took another sip anyway. If he thought about the flavor, maybe he could forget the fact that he was sitting here, drinking bad coffee, doing nothing to help find Tillette.

Kenzie stirred. Cole poured a fresh cup of coffee for her and took it to the couch.

"Nice nap?" He smiled at her tousled hair and unfocused gaze. She smiled back, a slow, soft curving of the lips that drew his eyes. He wanted to kiss her again—feel the warmth of her skin.

His cell phone rang. Cole set Kenzie's coffee on a coaster and checked the phone's screen. Parker.

"Leighton, you got Miss Jacobs with you?"

"She's here."

Kenzie's eyes lost their soft glow, and her smile tightened into a thin line.

Cole turned away from her. "What's going on?"

"Tillette—he's gone underground."

Monday, and still no sign of Tillette. They'd traced him to a hotel in downtown Atlanta, but he hadn't stayed there in days. All they knew was they couldn't find the guy, and tonight she was scheduled to be kidnapped.

Kenzie dug the knife in harder. She had to do something to whittle her time away.

Groaning, she twisted the wood in her hands. Not only were her jokes getting worse, she thought, but the pine wasn't cooperating. But she'd get it, even if she had to carve up a whole forest to figure it out.

"Is it going okay?"

Kenzie jumped at Cole's voice and shoved her work under a blanket. "You didn't peek, did you?"

"Well…"

She turned and glared as Cole sidled up beside her.

"Peek at what?" He reached for the block of wood, but she slapped his hand away and choked on a giggle.

The door swung open, and John entered the apartment. "Anyone up for Chinese?" Grocery bags rustled as John set his stash on the table.

The tension of the past ten days had Kenzie's moods zooming up and down like a roller coaster. Now was up. Way up—looking into Cole's eyes, teasing him and his cousin, knowing Cole cared for her enough to be willing to die to keep her safe…

And then she came crashing down, knowing Cole might end up doing just that.

In three hours, at 4:00 p.m., Kenzie Jacobs would head to

the gym. Except it wouldn't be Kenzie going into that building—Detective Parker had changed that much—and when her double came back out, only God knew what would happen next.

Cole watched as Officer Brittany Smithers, wearing Kenzie's clothes and a shiny brunette wig, stepped out of the apartment bathroom. She did look like Kenzie at first glance, maybe even second. But that didn't help him shake the sick and inexplicable feeling that this wasn't going to work.

Kenzie, now wearing a straight blond wig and Brittany's street clothes, moved to Cole's side. In just a few moments they would part ways. He mentally traced Brittany's steps— down the hall, into the elevator, out into the late afternoon where the sky was darkening with cloud cover. She'd climb into Kenzie's Accord and drive to the women's-only gym. Just over half an hour later, she'd come back out. Walk toward the car. And the team would grab whoever tried to take her. She'd be the instrument that ended Kenzie's nightmare.

If nothing went wrong.

Meanwhile, Parker had forbidden Cole to be anywhere near the scene. So he'd stay at the apartment, twiddling his thumbs and wishing he was in on the action. Kenzie, accompanied by Brittany's plainclothes partner, would drive the blonde's Jetta back to the station and stay tucked away until it was all over. Just another hour or so. Cole wrapped Kenzie in a tight hug. She'd be safe. And then she'd be free.

Kenzie pulled back and looked up into his face. Her eyes were dark, her expression taut. "Cole…" She began slowly, but then the words poured out. "I love orange soda—too much time with first-graders, I guess. I sometimes have nightmares. I'm deathly afraid of tornadoes. I used to eat ice cream on the porch with my dad. He died of a heart attack when I was fourteen, and I haven't eaten ice cream since. I have to turn my head when anyone's getting a shot—even on a movie. I love the colors blue and brown, and while we were in Kansas I finally figured out that my mother really does love me, and that I've been wrong about God for a very long time."

Cole bent farther for a clear view of her. Kenzie bit her lip, but kept her eyes shut. "What do you mean?" he said. "What have you been wrong about?"

"He loves me, too." She lowered her head; her hair tumbled around her face.

He felt the weight of the moment but couldn't fathom the significance. "Zee, why are you telling me all this?"

Her eyes, shining with unshed tears, finally opened and met his. Her free hand brushed across his cheek, tracing the line of his jaw. "I'm taking down a few more walls."

Cole needed to shave. Again. The stubble formed a dark shadow and rasped under Kenzie's fingers. She studied it, liking his five o'clock shadow, then moved on to touch his determined chin. His character was summed up in his face: stubborn jaw, gentle eyes, broad forehead that hinted at intelligence and wayward hair.

"What are you saying?" he finally whispered, warm gaze studying her intensely.

"I'm saying that…" She wanted to say the words, to taste them. But they opened her up to the possibility of more hurt and loss. Made her vulnerable. Was she ready for that? Did she really want that?

Cole ran a hand down her arm and cupped her elbow. "Tell me, Zee."

It was time to let go. To truly trust God, and to trust Cole. "I think I love you."

He blinked, and a shiver—the good kind—raced through her as she watched his eyes search hers, light up…focus on her lips.

"May I?" His breath fanned across her face as he leaned closer.

She forced herself to ignore their audience and managed a nod. Closed her eyes. Felt his lips touch, then take hers. Kenzie melted in the moment, then it was over. He pulled away, and she slid her hand to his chest, over the pounding of his heart.

"We haven't known each other long, but…I love you, Kenzie. More than I can tell you. But you know my past…" Pain filled his voice, along with a note of something else. Hope?

"I know it's the *past*." Her breath hitched.

He looked away, then back again, wearing a tender expression. He ran a thumb over her lips, then tucked a loose brown strand under her wig. She relished his touch, felt the loss when he pulled away.

Kenzie tugged him down until his forehead touched hers, then shifted to kiss him once again.

Brittany cleared her throat. Time to walk out that door and end all this. But for just a moment more, she wanted to savor this feeling.

Just in case something went wrong.

Kenzie followed the second officer—her "partner"—across the lot at the police station. The winds had picked up. A paper bag skittered across the pavement, then lifted into the air. Clouds rolled in, each layer darker than the other. The rain had let up some, but if she had her guess, it would come again. Hopefully they'd have at least thirty minutes more before the fury hit.

A tremor coursed through her, but she shoved it down. Only some rain, and there was still a glimpse of sun. She had to concentrate on this moment and the ones to follow.

Inside the station, Kenzie settled near Dorothy, an older African-American woman with close-cut curls and a grim smile. If anything went wrong, or if Parker needed Kenzie for anything, Dorothy was there to take care of it. And to take care of her, Kenzie assumed. The combination of tough lady and grandma that made up Dorothy's persona helped Kenzie believe she could do it.

That maybe this would go down okay, after all.

Cole gripped his mug, even though it was empty. The apartment was too quiet. He checked the clock again—the third time in as many minutes. Brittany wouldn't be stepping outside the gym for at least another seven minutes.

Which called for another cup of coffee.

He should be praying, but his nerves were too jittery to concentrate. His words all circled back to one thought and not much else: *God, please help*.

Thunder rumbled, rattling the pictures on the wall. As the lights flickered, Cole shifted his eyes toward the couch before remembering Kenzie wasn't there. Hopefully at the police station she didn't have a view of the worsening storm. She would be terrified of it.

It would be okay. She was in good hands.

Still clutching his mug, Cole settled onto the couch. If he angled away from the clock, maybe time could go by faster. A blanket slid off the leather and landed with a muffled *clunk*. Cole glanced down and remembered how Kenzie had shoved the block of wood underneath it. He'd wanted to watch her work—her deft strokes with the knife, the way her brow furrowed in concentration. But he'd only caught a glimpse of her before she'd turned away from him, firmly instructing him not to look.

But she wasn't here now. He'd stand for a scolding if it meant she would come back to him, safe from the man making a mess of her life.

He scooped up the blanket and unwrapped its folds. The wood still looked squarish, the lines rough and incomplete. But there, in the heart of the block, nestled a woman, held tightly to a man's heart.

The drawing from his sketchbook.

He gently traced the shape. He should never have let her go. When they were together next, he wanted to study her hands, see how many nicks she'd gotten over the years, rub the calluses that had formed from years of whittling—

He checked the clock and straightened. Showtime.

Kenzie leaned against the wall at the station, trying not to hyperventilate. The storm was too much; the dark was going to claim her. But it couldn't. Not now. Not when Brittany was about to walk out of the building and—

Her eyes flew open.

—and into the storm. Which would make anyone who had been watching the real Kenzie Jacobs for any amount of time realize that the woman calmly striding across the parking lot amid terrible lightning and crashing thunder and pelting rain was not *her*. The real Kenzie would stay inside the building, huddled against a wall, reacting to each bolt of lightning as if it had entered her body. Maybe she'd fall down into her dark place—the place where she was slowly sliding now.

Nothing could have made her walk out into the storm.

"Call Parker!" she shouted to the room in general. "Tell everyone to stop!"

Dorothy swept up the radio, relaying the message in an even but urgent tone. Then she handed the microphone over.

"Detective," Kenzie blurted out. "The storm—is it really bad there?"

"Miss Jacobs, we don't have time for this. Get to the point."

"If the storm is bad, and Brittany walks outside, Tillette will know she's not me!"

Silence.

"I'm terrified of storms, Detective Parker. If he's been watching me as much as we think he has, he'll know I wouldn't go outside until it calms down."

Her breath came in rapid gasps. She tried to force calm—breathing in through her nose, out through her mouth—and listened for the detective's answer.

"Too late," he finally said. "She was already stepping off the curb. We gotta go ahead. She's halfway to the car now."

Kenzie stepped back, nearly staggering under the weight of his words. Too late? She doubled over, hanging on to a chair to keep her on her feet. Dorothy's arms slid around her, but though they offered support, they failed to give comfort.

The nightmare wouldn't end tonight. Would it ever?

TWENTY-FOUR

Kenzie's phone rang. She lifted her head and pushed away from Dorothy. Maybe it was Cole. She needed him—

Not Cole. A number she didn't recognize. Her finger slid to accept the call. It could be Tillette. She had to answer.

"MacKenzie Jacobs?" Not Tillette's voice, but vaguely familiar.

"Mmm." The emptiness inside didn't lend itself to niceties.

"This is Warren Flint."

Kenzie nearly dropped the phone. She fumbled, held it back to her ear in time to hear, "I just want to say how sorry I am that my book—"

She found her voice as well as a nugget of anger. "I appreciate that, but I don't have the time right now, Mr. Flint."

"Listen. I think you need to hear this."

"Apologies aren't necessary. I agreed to the photo shoot. This is not your fault, so if you'll—"

"I found something. It might help."

Kenzie stilled at the somber note in his voice.

"Someone sent me a screenplay of my book a while back. They wanted my endorsement. I kept it—setting it aside to read when I got the time, but I forgot about it until Cole Leighton contacted me."

The point! Get to the point!

"So I read it, thinking it might help. And MacKenzie…there's a twist at the end."

Her teeth resumed chattering.

"Instead of Monique being taken a second time, the villain takes Evan, her lover. It's like he wears her down the entire time until, at the end when he takes her fiancé, she's ready to surrender without a fight just to get it over with. Is there—"

Thunder and police station chatter settled into a dull background roar as the words hit home. The trap would have failed anyway—all those people out there risking their lives in the storm, and Tillette probably hadn't even gone. But…maybe there was no connection. Coincidence.

"Mr. Flint," she interrupted. "Who wrote the script?"

"He's the one who read the story for the audiobook version. Luther Tillette. MacKenzie, I think—"

Her hands shook so hard it took three tries before she successfully hung up on the author. "Dorothy!" The secretary looked up from her desk as Kenzie fumbled over Cole's phone number. "Get Detective Parker again!"

Kenzie tapped her phone until the right number finally appeared. Pressed Send. It dialed, said it was calling…

Call failed. Retry.

Nothing.

Retry.

Cole, come on. A tear hit the buttons on the phone as the call failed again. Cole wasn't her lover or fiancé, but he was the closest thing she had. Tillette was going to grab him. Then Cole would be dead. Like Mikey.

Lights dimmed. Flickered. Failed. Thunder crashed closer. Kenzie sank lower against the wall, sliding down, sinking into the darkness.

* * *

Someone knocked on the door. Once. Twice. Three times. John wouldn't knock on his own door. Besides, he wasn't supposed to get home from work for another hour. Could Kenzie be back already? A smooth pickup? The news hadn't had any reports yet, but it was probably too soon for them to get anything on the air.

Cole swept the wood under the blanket, then bounded to the door and yanked it open. "How did it—?" He broke off and shoved against the door. Too slow.

Tillette stood before him. Smiling.

Cole jerked back. Stumbled. Almost caught himself. Then Tillette lifted a gun…

Fired.

Cole went stiff, then felt himself falling. Down. Down. And there was nothing he could do.

Cold seeped through her jeans. Her back ached from scrunching down so low, so long. Someone shook Kenzie, yelling her name. Where was Mikey? Was the tornado over?

"Kenzie!"

She lifted her head and blinked. The exit light glared gargoyle-red. Her hand hurt, and she relaxed it to find it imprinted with the outline of Mikey's pocketknife.

"There's a tornado warning! We need to get somewhere safe," Dorothy said.

Everything flooded back to her then. The trap. The storm. The screenplay.

Cole.

"I have to talk to Detective Parker!"

Dorothy came close and stared straight into her face. "A funnel has been sighted, Kenzie."

She squeezed her eyes closed, trying in vain to shut out the panic.

Dorothy tugged on Kenzie's arm. "Parker's first priority right now is the safety of his team. There's nothing we can do until the storm blows over except stay safe ourselves. C'mon, hon. Let's go."

Kenzie allowed herself to be guided deeper into the building, trusting Dorothy to lead her. The cop seemed strong, capable. Mikey might not be here, but Kenzie was in good hands.

But Cole might not be.

Kenzie stopped and pulled away. "Go ahead without me." There was something she had to do.

TWENTY-FIVE

Cole felt as if his body no longer existed. Only pain. He hit the ground and tried to move, but he was on fire. When the buzzing finally ended, Tillette wrapped duct tape around Cole's wrists before he could react.

Cole kicked with his legs. Failed to connect as his brain refused to clear. Then the buzzing came again from the Taser. This time when it ended, Cole remained still, gasping for breath.

"Rest there a while," Tillette said, binding his ankles, then closing the door. "You'll need your strength for what's coming next."

Good news—since Tillette was here, Kenzie was safe for the moment. The bad news was that the trap had obviously failed…and now Cole was the one ensnared.

"What do you want?" The lingering pain tightened Cole's throat, altering the tenor of his voice.

"MacKenzie Jacobs. But I think you already knew that, true?" Tillette slanted him a look.

"Why?" Cole moved his feet. His muscles ached but were slowly coming back to life. "Haven't you terrorized her enough?"

A slow smile spread across Tillette's face. "No. Not quite."

* * *

Rain fell in sheets, rendering the windshield wipers useless. Kenzie tapped the accelerator, groaning with impatience as Brittany's Jetta struggled through the wind and water at just over ten miles an hour.

She'd never make it to Cole at this rate. She could almost swim faster. *God, please. Don't let anyone else die for me.*

The wall of water continually washed over the car. Kenzie felt herself shrinking, huddling in her seat like she was a little girl again, crouched in a corner of the basement, waiting an eerie eternity for Mikey to come back through that door. Or for it to fly open and allow entry to something else entirely…the same something that sucked the roof off the house and left only splintered remains. The same something that picked up her brother and flung him to his death.

Her breathing became sporadic as thunder crescendoed. The rain abruptly ceased. Overhead hung black clouds with a layer of angry green.

Kenzie sensed the hunger of the storm—it was coming for her. And this time she had to face it alone.

No, not alone. With the One Who saw every sparrow that fell from its nest.

God, please don't let me fall. No otherworldly voice filled the vehicle. Only a solid *thunk* as something hit the windshield. Then four more in rapid succession. Hail.

Only a few blocks from John's apartment.

Kenzie drove on, aiming the car into the mouth of the storm.

Thunder rumbled through the building, vibrating Cole's back. No light streamed through the open blinds. The darkness felt almost as heavy as Cole's useless body. How was Kenzie handling it?

Stay safe, Zee. God, cover her with Your hand. He tried to move his legs, to wrestle a bit of give in his restraints with little success.

Cole cleared his throat and mouthed a couple words before giving speech another try. "So now what?" His voice was weak but had no whine in evidence, thankfully. Even when he'd lost control of everything else, he'd managed to keep his groans of pain inside.

Tillette didn't turn away from the window. "Now we finish the story."

"*Obsession*?"

"Yes."

Cole flexed his hands. Stronger. "But I've read the book. This wasn't in it."

"No," Tillette said. His accent was very distinct though easily understood. "Not the book. The screenplay." He finally swung his gaze from the window.

Cole's blood ran cold. "Screenplay?"

Tillette smiled. "It has a killer ending."

With hail the size of pebbles still pelting the windshield, Kenzie pivoted the car half onto the deserted sidewalk in front of John's building. She took the few feet to the entryway at a mad dash, then halted inside the lobby. The lights flickered once, then again as she paused by the elevator, wondering whether to chance using it. Maybe she'd make it up to Cole faster...maybe she'd die of fear after being trapped between floors.

A couple of residents scuttled by, heading down a short hallway and disappearing around a corner. Did the building have a safe room?

Shivering from more than the cold, Kenzie headed for the stairs. Her clothes dripped rainwater, leaving a trail across the tile floor, then on the concrete block as she mounted the first flight of steps. Peering up through the center, she could see the railing circle higher and higher. She only had to climb halfway, to the fifth floor. Then she'd be with Cole, know he was safe, and maybe that would be enough to ward off the storm raging inside and out.

A small window should have lit the landing; instead, it allowed the suffocating darkness to invade. She planted her foot on the first step of the second flight, then halted when the patter outside died away. The window drew her back as dread icier than the hail slammed into her. The sudden quietness could mean the storm was over…or that it had only begun.

Touching the glass, Kenzie watched as wind stretched the trees. A metal garbage can rolled by. Her skin prickled. Every nerve screamed to go down, find shelter, burrow into a concrete cocoon as the rest of the world blew away.

But Cole was upstairs.

And there in the parking lot, a silver Lincoln sat empty.

She started to turn, ready to run the next four flights, screaming for Cole the entire way. Then in the distance—dark motion. Black wisps of clouds circled on the dance floor of the sky. Closer. Closer. Then together in a tight formation, they dropped. A car swirled once and disappeared. The black mouth raised, skipped over a tree or two, then lowered for another bite.

Luther Tillette's good humor died with the lights. In the darkness, Cole was jerked to his feet. A blade sliced through the tape on his ankles, and he flinched as it nicked him through his sock. At least his feet were free.

"Change of plans," Tillette growled. "We're going to take a little trip."

Cole stumbled to the door as hard metal in his back propelled him forward, into the hallway bathed in the dim red
light of the exit signs. Down the hall in the opposite direction
of the elevator. Wrists still tightly bound behind his back,
Tillette's guiding hand on his shoulder and gun pressing
against the base of his neck, Cole reached the door to the
stairs. He hit the bar hard with his stomach, and the door
banged open. Five flights of stairs in the dark. He could use
this to his advantage.

Four flights.

The air changed; Cole's ears popped. But the change in
atmosphere did nothing to release the pressure of Tillette's
gun.

Three flights.

Tillette pushed for greater speed, and his breath came in
heavy bursts. From fear, or was he out of shape? Cole tensed,
but so did the gun.

Two flights.

Cole missed a step off the landing and one knee buckled.
The gun slipped. Cole jerked backward, ramming his body
into his captor's. They both went down hard as metal skidded,
clanged, then hushed for a long moment before a final clatter
echoed from far below.

Tillette lunged, crushing Cole with his weight. Cole
twisted. His hands were useless, but he shoved with his feet,
and Tillette crashed against the railing halfway down the
flight of steps.

She was going to die here, in this tornado. It would suck
her up from the first floor landing and deposit her lifeless
body somewhere far away, stealing her from Cole in the same
way it had taken Mikey from her.

God!

As the last rays of light outside began to fade, Kenzie fought the darkness as it sought to envelope her mind. Her breath came in shallow gasps. But she would not give in. Punishment wasn't inevitable. She didn't have a target hanging over her head. She was beloved by her Father in heaven. She would not let this storm win. She'd trust God this time.

And get away from the window.

"Kenzie!"

She spun at the sound of Cole's voice and made out Tillette's form in the murky shadows, rushing toward her. She jumped back, landed in a puddle. Twisted and fell. Tillette's meaty hand gripped her throat and pulled. Choking, Kenzie scrambled for footing and heaved herself upward, fighting for air. She tried to kick, but her right ankle screamed in pain from the fall and wouldn't hold her weight. Buckling slightly, she lost her air flow.

Cole!

Through watery eyes, she finally spotted him, hunched on the steps. Hurt? Or just helpless, with Tillette using her as a threat?

She clawed at the fingers gripping her throat. A thin trickle of oxygen broke through the barricade. She gasped it down and fought for more. Her ears roared—from the fight or the storm? Couldn't Tillette sense the twister's approach?

Her hands loosened on his as darkness began to close in.

Down, down. Mikey had led her lower, deep into the shadowed safety of the basement. He'd left her there. But his knife had stayed with her.

Kenzie jerked alert. The knife.

TWENTY-SIX

Anguish crushed Cole's lungs as he watched Kenzie struggle. With every instinct screaming to attack, he waited for Tillette to withdraw the Taser from its hiding place. He needed to know where the weapon was, to fight against it, to avoid it so as not to be rendered helpless, with Kenzie in the hands of a maniac.

But Tillette didn't pull out the weapon, and Kenzie was being strangled by those hands.

Before Cole could lunge, something flashed at Kenzie's side. A deft flick of her wrist, a short jab at her captor's leg, then Tillette let out a yell and dropped her to the floor.

Cole sprang, covering the final steps in one long leap, then once again used his body as a battering ram. Tillette stumbled, dropped and crashed down the stairs.

A roar filled the staircase, deep and guttural like a freight train. Kenzie's icy fingers met Cole's arm and tightened into a death grip as she yanked him toward where Tillette had fallen.

"Kenzie!" Cole hung back trying to point her toward the exit. "Let's get out of here!" They should just leave Tillette for the police to deal with. He needed to get Kenzie away from here.

But Kenzie jerked harder. "Are you crazy? Come on!" Her hobbling steps were punctuated by cries of agony.

"Hold up, Zee." The roar grew so loud that he couldn't think straight.

Then glass exploded, and thinking no longer mattered. Only getting down below.

Kenzie felt the air snap and pop as they fled the remaining distance to the unfamiliar basement. Cole slammed the door behind them. He led her away from it, around a corner to an inside wall.

She sliced at his bindings with Mikey's knife, trying not to gag at the blade, slick with Tillette's blood. Then Cole jerked her down against the wall and wrapped her in a protective embrace.

"It's okay," he shouted over the storm's fury. "I'm not going to leave you, Zee. We're going to be okay." While it whipped up the world outside, everything inside moved at a snail's pace. Kenzie pressed closer to Cole, focusing on his heart and trying to match its steady rhythm with the beat of her own.

The door rattled. Cole held her tight, and as glass shattered in the distance, he pressed his mouth to her hair. With her head on his shoulder, Kenzie soaked up the comfort of his voice, his touch. The storm, the darkness—it felt different this time—better, even though a more personal danger lurked outside the door. The fear made her limbs tremble, but didn't control her mind. She didn't want to die, but knew she'd be in a better place if she did.

She was loved. She was never alone. That made everything all right.

Almost.

Heavier than the air, eerie silence filled the basement. Cole tightened his arm around Kenzie, bending to try to see her face. Too dark; he saw only shadow. But she was breathing okay, and, though she shook slightly, she didn't whimper as her chilled fingertips cupped his cheek.

"Thank you," she whispered.

"What are you doing here, Zee?" She should still be safe at the police station, not braving twisters and evil gunmen.

"I'm waiting out a storm with the man I love."

He smiled, turning his head to kiss the palm of her hand. He didn't deserve her love—another gift of grace. "Let's get out of here safely, then we'll find somewhere to talk about us."

"Good idea." There was a smile in her voice. Then she was kissing him, her mouth covering his, stealing his breath and threatening to never return it.

Reluctantly, he broke away and stood, tugging her up with him. They needed to go. If they could find another exit—

A hammer clicked, quiet but deadly. "This wasn't the setting I had planned for the final act," Tillette rasped, his accent thickening. "But I think this could do quite nicely."

Cole turned to face the enemy, holding Kenzie behind him. It couldn't end here. Not like this. They'd come too far. "Don't you think you've played your little game long enough? This isn't a movie. We're not actors. Whatever happens here, you can't push the rewind button."

Tillette ignored him. "The script is upstairs, so we'll have to wing it. But you've been doing quite a bit of that, and I like the changes, so let's just see how this turns out."

"What if you don't like the ending?" Cole tightened his grip on Kenzie's arms.

"Then I'll start over."

Kenzie kept quiet, mind racing as Cole's fingers dug into her arms. His lean body blocked hers, protecting her the best he could. Always the hero. But this was her fight—she was the intended prey. She was the one who should be offering herself as a shield. But how?

Please, God. A little wisdom. "So what is supposed to happen?" she asked. "Because it'll be hard to act it out if we don't have a clue what you have in mind."

Oh, right. Get him talking, listen to him confess and eventually some way of escape would open up. How...unlikely.

The dirty windows let in a little more light now, enough to see the dark stain on his pant leg where she'd stabbed him, the sprinkling of glass and debris on his shoulders and the way his eyes narrowed. Not at her, but at the room. Judging how best to end this, probably—where he wanted his pawns to play the last role of their lives.

"MacKenzie, you surprised me. I didn't think you'd have any fight left. I thought you'd be ready to surrender so the nightmare would finally end—"

She'd been close. So close. If it weren't for Cole. And God...

"—but you continually add twists I hadn't anticipated."

While Kenzie waited, wondering what to make of that, Luther Tillette came closer, his weapon aimed at Cole's chest. She had a feeling he wouldn't miss his mark. The bullet would kill Cole—maybe her, too. They needed to separate. Get an edge on the creep.

She pulled back, prying Cole's fingers off her arms. "So why don't you let us go? We can do the cat-and-mouse thing until we're both tired of it, then go our different ways." Of course, his path would involve a metal cage with the key thrown away if she had anything to do with it.

He chuckled—an ominous sound that echoed off the dank walls. "Sorry, pet."

As she hobbled away from Cole, Luther pinned her with

his frosty stare. How was it possible that such a handsome face could hide such evil?

Cole tried to step in front of her again, but Luther waved him away. Out of the corner of her eye, Kenzie saw Cole's muscles tense.

"Why is Cole a part of this?" Kenzie asked. Maybe she could distract Luther long enough for Cole to have a chance. Or maybe Cole would sense from the tension in her voice that he needed to wait. Luther was ready—a panther waiting to pounce.

"The man you love is good bait. And the best one to pin this on, true? I wrote the script with your coach friend in mind, but even in that area you managed to surprise me."

Coach Bryan? Cole slanted her a look. If she weren't so terrified, she'd have a little fun with that, try to make him jealous. But there was no one she'd rather have beside her. For now. Maybe for eternity.

And yet…anyone *but* him. If he got hurt—

She closed her eyes, trying to block Mikey's image.

"So in this scene—" Luther took a step, then broke off and motioned for Cole to take a seat. Cole did—slowly, reluctantly— and Luther continued. "MacKenzie, why don't you sit over there." He pointed to the floor next to Cole. So much for splitting up.

In the book, Monique lived. But Warren Flint said the ending had changed. Why hadn't she stayed on the phone long enough to find out what happened? The chill in the room came from more than the wind blowing over the fallen hail outside, the dampness of her clothing. She knew it then, just looking at him. His version of Monique would die, and Evan/Cole would die with her.

"Mr. Leighton, you want to live, no?"

"Yes."

"No true, you love her?"

"Yes," Cole said again without hesitation.

"If you had your preference…would you rather watch her die a slow, painful death before you are killed?"

Kenzie drew in a long breath as she waited for the alternative.

"Or would you rather pull the trigger yourself and walk away free?"

After the shock of that, Kenzie nudged Cole. Was she missing something? If Luther gave up his gun, what could he do to them? She had a twisted ankle, but Luther had a knife wound in his leg—they'd be even in a chase, right?

"Think about it," Luther said, then withdrew something from the pocket of his jacket—the shadowy shape of another weapon.

TWENTY-SEVEN

Kenzie slumped against the wall. Cole felt the defeat radiating from her. She'd faced her worst fear—survived another tornado—but this storm seemed never ending. How long until she just gave up?

She wouldn't. She was stronger than that. But was he? If he had to choose between allowing her to be tortured—watching it, feeling each moment of agony along with Kenzie—or ending her life himself, which would it be? What would be the lesser of two evils? Killing Kenzie would be worse than death for him. Watching her suffer would be equally intolerable.

He wouldn't do either. Couldn't. He'd jump Tillette, allow the bullets to rip him in two and hope he'd bought enough time for Kenzie to flee. His heart was shredding anyway. The rest should match. He'd go out the hero he'd always wanted to be…

If Kenzie managed to escape. If not, his sacrifice would be worse than useless—it would leave her utterly defenseless.

"You have one minute to decide," Tillette said. The man backed away, then stood, casually studying the barrel of the gun as the seconds ticked by.

One minute. Fifty seconds. Forty-five seconds until Cole would choose which way either or both of them would die.

Kenzie's body shuddered against his, but no sobs escaped. Instead, he heard her whispering, "Yea, though I walk through the valley of the shadow of death, I will fear no evil, for thou art with me."

Thirty seconds. His mind blanked, refusing to make any decisions.

Fifteen seconds. His heart thudded hard against his ribs. He'd give his life for hers. But how?

Five seconds. Tillette glanced at his watch.

"Give Cole the gun," Kenzie said, her voice strong. "He'll do it."

Cole stiffened. "Zee—"

Her eyes flashed at him. No arguing. There was a message in their dark-blue depths. She held his gaze, blinked once and nodded. He nodded back.

Kenzie fumbled in her pocket and punched Redial on her cell phone, as she had periodically ever since Luther had walked in on them. The 911 calls probably weren't going through—the tornado had probably messed up the system, but still…

She finally recognized the other weapon. A Taser. She'd never seen one in real life, but she'd heard about them, seen their effects on television. If Cole tried something and didn't put Luther Tillette out of commission immediately, Cole would be tased, leaving him helpless.

She shuddered. What were their chances? With a weapon on their side…if Cole were hurt and dropped the gun, she could try her own hand at it.

It seemed too risky…which meant Luther must have something else up his sleeve. Maybe literally.

He wore a sly smile. "So here is how we're going to do this."

Cole shifted his position slightly, ready to jump at any promising instant.

"MacKenzie, I need you to—"

A siren blared. Luther twisted his upper body toward the high window where red-and-blue lights flashed. Then Kenzie hit the floor as Cole shoved and lunged. Kenzie rolled and came up fast, ignoring her throbbing ankle as she searched wildly for something to use as a weapon. Empty bucket and a mop. Tall stacks of boxes.

A hiss of electricity—the Taser. She heard a groan, turned to see Cole down, writhing in pain. Luther stepped toward her, smiling. The gun came up slowly...

Lift your eyes to the hills.

She raised her gaze, saw the paint cans seconds before she slammed into the metal shelving. The shelf rocked, and two cans slid free, one landing a glancing blow on Luther's head. He staggered as she rushed to ram the boxes next. They teetered, then cascaded down just as he brought the gun to bear.

And as two uniformed officers swept into the room.

A shot rang out. Kenzie waited for the blow, but it never came. The weapon fell from Tillette's hands, and he collapsed into the pile of boxes with a moan. The cops moved in, snapping cuffs on their new prisoner and securing the area as Detective Parker charged into the basement.

Kenzie felt her legs give out beneath her and dropped to her knees. The voices mingled, the room blurred and spun around her. And then trembling arms gathered her up and cradled her close. She shut her eyes and hugged Cole tight, burying her face in his neck.

It was over. Finally.

TWENTY-EIGHT

Kenzie's tremors were finally starting to fade, but the tears leaked out periodically as she clung to Cole. They both gave their statements, were examined by the paramedics and were finally told they could go.

Outside, they sat on the sidewalk near the entrance, soaking in the sun as it finally made an appearance. Kenzie propped her wrapped ankle on a parking stop and leaned against Cole. The apartment building had been damaged but not demolished. Some trees uprooted. Cars destroyed. A few houses. No lives had been lost as far as the authorities knew.

Cole seemed fine now. Alive and in love with her, if his adoring eyes were any indication. She hadn't thought anyone would ever look at her like that; she liked it…a lot.

"There's something I can't figure out," she said. "If everything works together for a purpose…"

Cole chuckled. "Maybe we're not meant to know."

"Well, I'm thinking we wouldn't have gotten to know each other if it weren't for Luther Tillette and his 'obsession.'"

A mock grimace crossed Cole's face. "And this is the story you're going to tell our children when they ask how we met?"

Her heart stopped at the word *children,* then skipped to double time. By the close attention he was giving her, she figured that had been the intention. She didn't give him the satisfaction of a gooey-eyed reaction. "It's exciting, at least."

"True, but they might have nightmares."

"We'll give them an edited version until they're old enough to handle it."

Cole's eyes danced, but he played along, maintaining a serious expression. "That's one option. But how about this one—why don't we just start over?"

Kenzie grimaced in the direction Luther Tillette had disappeared earlier on a stretcher. "Sounds…dangerous."

"No, I mean…" He stopped. Picked up her hand and placed a lingering kiss on her scraped knuckles. "My name is Cole Leighton. I couldn't help noticing you sitting on the sidewalk—couldn't look away, actually. Will you go to dinner with me?"

She hesitated, biting back a smile. "I don't know…I mean, you could be a stalker or something."

His mouth twitched slightly. "I see. So you'd like to get to know me a little better first?"

She laughed and tried to cut him off, but he ticked off his name, address and enough information about himself that she could rob him of everything he owned.

"Now can we go to dinner?"

"Well…"

His mouth twitched again, and a half smile escaped. She studied him as he talked, the soft timbre of his voice comforting something deep inside as he held her hand tightly between both of his. As if he would never let go.

She loved this man. Now that the drama was over, they could have more times like these—laughter, teasing and kissing and enjoying each other's company.

But what if he went back to Texas? With the danger over,

he had no real reason to stay. His job was waiting for him. His life...

She didn't notice he'd stopped talking until she realized how intently he was studying her.

"You're not going to say anything?" he finally asked.

"What?"

He stared a moment longer, then let out a low-throated chuckle. "You weren't paying attention, were you?"

Heat filled her face. "Um..."

Cole laughed harder. "Well, that's not quite how I thought that would go."

She winced. "What did I miss?"

"Not much. Just something like this—" He moved to kneel in front of her, still hanging on to her hand. "Will you marry me?"

Her breath caught. Could he really love her that much? Enough to commit to forever? Cole would have died for her back in the basement. What greater love was there?

"Um, Zee?"

"Hmm?"

"You did hear me this time, right?"

A smile covered her face, stretching so far it almost hurt. "I heard you."

His eyes anxiously scanned her face, begging for an answer.

"Yes." How could one word hold so much promise?

Cole leaned closer, and his kiss nearly stopped her heart again. "When?" he asked, pulling back just enough for her to be able to focus on his handsome, dirt-streaked face.

Kenzie smiled and touched his lips with hers, glancing over his shoulder to Detective Parker where he spoke with a couple of officers. "Why don't we see if the detective can perform the ceremony when he's done here?"

Cole smiled into her eyes, his gaze turning incredibly soft. "Why don't we wait until you don't have to hobble down the aisle?" He gently touched her bandaged ankle.

"So…next week, same time?" She didn't want to miss one moment of Cole's life—not a thing. Not after she'd almost lost him altogether.

"Deal." He winked and sat beside her again, draping his arm around her shoulders. His body heat warmed her skin through her clothing.

"Good." She leaned into him. "I'll bring the dress. You bring the flowers."

"No roses, right?"

A tremor passed through her body, then was gone. "Something bright—gerbera daisies or sunflowers, maybe."

"Sunflowers. Perfect."

They would be. They were made for the sun, tracking its movement across the sky, keeping their faces to the light. "Sunflowers it is."

Cole kissed her temple, then rested his cheek against her head. "I love you, MacKenzie Jacobs."

"Really?"

His rough jaw scraped against her face as he nodded.

"Maybe you should prove it sometime." She bit her lip as he slowly leaned away far enough to see her eyes. Then she lifted her face to the sky and let the laughter spill over.

Thank You, God.

Cole stood, and she wrapped her arms around his waist and limped beside him. They passed Tillette's Town Car. A bouquet of roses rested on the passenger seat. His final gift? Kenzie pressed against the window to read the name on the card.

Amy.

She blinked.

"He already had his next victim picked out," Cole said, a note of disbelief in his voice.

"The ending of his script?"

Cole held her close. "Or the beginning of a new one."

Kenzie shivered, then shook it off and led the way past the vehicle. "But it's the end of *this* story."

Cole kissed the top of her head. Paused. Then repeated, "And the beginning of a new one."

* * * * *

Dear Reader,

Thank you so much for allowing me to share Cole and Kenzie's story with you. I hope you enjoyed their journey toward finding God's love and forgiveness. Remember that you are God's beloved creation, and there is nothing He cannot forgive—no stain too dark for His blood to wash clean.

I loved writing this book and would love to hear from my readers. You can reach me through my Web site at: www.jennesswalker.com, or in care of Steeple Hill Books, 233 Broadway, Suite 1001, New York, NY 10279.

May God bless you, and may you continue to draw closer to Him.

Jenness Walker

QUESTIONS FOR DISCUSSION

1. For much of the story, Cole feels like he will never be good enough to deserve God's forgiveness for his past. Have you ever felt that way? Or that you have to earn God's forgiveness?

2. Kenzie built walls around her heart so that she wouldn't be hurt by losing someone again. What did this do to her relationship with others? With God?

3. How did Kenzie's actions help Cole understand his relationship with Jesus better?

4. The storms in Kenzie's life left her emotionally scarred and fatalistic. Why? How did accepting God's love help her to face her fears?

5. Kenzie had a rocky relationship with her mother. Instead of giving up on Kenzie, what do you think Eleanor should have done to reach her?

6. Kenzie thought that when bad things happened to her, that meant God didn't love her. Have you ever felt this way?

7. Kenzie finally realized that she was loved. She was beloved by the God Who knew everything about her, even the number of hairs on her head. Do you know God loves you, His child? How does that knowledge change you?

8. Do you relate to either Cole or Kenzie? Which one? Why?

9. Even when it meant he looked crazy, Cole stood up for what he thought was right and tried to help Kenzie. Have you ever had to do this? Or did you give in and do the easy thing? Did you learn anything from your decisions?

10. Kenzie had many dark moments when fear took over. What are you most afraid of? Does the fear ever paralyze you? If so, how do you overcome it? What helped Kenzie face her fears in the end?

11. Kenzie was afraid to let Cole love her and tried to protect him by running away. Do you think she did the right thing? Why or why not?

12. The book talks about accepting the fact that you are loved and can be forgiven. Do you find this easy or hard to accept? Why?

13. Kenzie didn't have a good relationship with her mother. Kenzie reacted by refusing to let her loved ones into her heart. How are your relationships? Could allowing yourself to be vulnerable mend a relationship?

14. Have you ever had your home invaded or in some other way felt your security had been violated? How did that make you feel? How did you overcome it?

15. Kenzie and Cole both benefited by sharing their internal problems with each other. Do you have anyone you can share your burdens with? How do you think this could help?

When a young Roman woman is wrenched from the safety of her family and sold into slavery, she finds herself at the mercy of the most famous gladiator in Rome. In God's plan, a master and his slave just might fall in love....

Turn the page for a sneak preview of
THE GLADIATOR
by Carla Capshaw
Available in November 2009
from Love Inspired® Historical

Rome, 81 A.D.

Angry, unfamiliar voices penetrated Pelonia's awareness. Floating between wakefulness and dark, she couldn't budge. Every muscle ached. A sharp pain drummed against her skull.

The voices died away, then a woman's words broke through the haze.

"My name is Lucia. Can you hear me?" The woman pressed a cup of water to Pelonia's cracked lips. "What shall I call you?"

Pelonia coughed as the cool liquid trickled down her arid throat. "Pel...Pelonia."

"Do you remember what happened to you? You were struck on the head and injured. I've been giving you opium to soothe you, but you're far from recovered."

Her eyelids too heavy to open, Pelonia licked her chapped lips.

Gradually her mind began to make sense of her surroundings. The warmth must be sunshine, because the scent of wood smoke hung in the air. Her pallet was a coarse woolen blanket on the hard ground. Dirt clung to her skin and each of her sore muscles longed for the softness of her bed at home.

Home.

Where was she if not in the comfort of her father's Umbrian villa? Who was this woman Lucia? She couldn't remember.

Icy fingers of fear gripped her heart as one by one her memories returned. First the attack, then her father's murder. Raw grief squeezed her chest.

Confusion surrounded her. Where was her uncle? She remembered the slave caravan, his threat to sell her, but nothing more.

Panic forced her eyes open. She managed to focus on the young woman's face above her.

"The master will be here soon." A smile tilted Lucia's thin lips, but didn't touch her honey-brown eyes.

"Where…am I?" she asked, the words grating in her throat.

"You're in the home of Caros Viriathos."

The name meant nothing to Pelonia. She prayed God had delivered her into the hands of a kind man, someone who would help her contact her cousin Tiberia.

Her eyes closed with fatigue. "How…how long have I…been here?"

"Four days and this morning. You've been in and out of sleep. I'll order you a bowl of broth. You should eat to bolster your strength."

Four days, and she remembered nothing. Tiberia must be frantic wondering why she'd failed to attend her wedding.

She opened her eyes. "I must—"

"Don't speak. Now that you've woken, Gaius, our master's steward, says you have one week to recover. Then your labor begins."

"My cousin. I must…"

"You're a slave in the Ludus Maximus now. A possession of the *lanista,* Caros Viriathos."

Lanista? A vile *gladiator* trainer?

"No!"

Lucia crossed her arms over her buxom chest. "We will see."

Heavy footsteps crunched on the rushes strewn across the floor. The new arrival stopped out of Pelonia's view.

The nauseating ache in her head increased without mercy. What had she done to make God despise her?

Focusing on Lucia, she saw the young woman's face light with pleasure.

"Master," Lucia greeted, jumping to her feet. "The new slave is finally awake. She calls herself Pelonia. She's weak and the medicine I gave her has run its course."

"Then give her more if she needs it."

The man's deep voice poured over Pelonia like the soothing water of a bath. She turned her head, ignoring the jab of pain that pierced her skull.

"You mustn't move your head," Lucia snapped, "or you might injure yourself further."

Pelonia stiffened. She wasn't accustomed to taking orders from slaves.

Lucia glanced toward the door. "She's argumentative. I have a hunch she'll be difficult. She denies she's your slave."

Silence followed Lucia's remark. Would this man who claimed to own her kill or beat her? Was he a cruel barbarian?

She sensed him move closer. Her tension rose as if she were prey in the sights of a hungry lion. At last the lion crossed to where she could see him.

Sunlight streaming through the window enveloped the giant, giving his dark hair a golden glow. A crisp, light-colored tunic draped across his shoulders and chest contrasted sharply with the rich copper of his skin. Gold bands around his upper arms emphasized the thickness of his muscles, the physical power he held in check.

Her breath hitched in her throat. She could only stare. Without a doubt, the man could crush her if he chose.

"So, you are called Pelonia," he said. "And my healer believes you wish to fight me."

Her gaze locked with the unusual blue of his forceful glare. For the first time she understood how the Hebrew, David, must have suffered when he faced Goliath. Swallowing the lump of fear in her throat, she nodded. "If I must."

"If you must?" Caros eyed Pelonia with a mix of irritation and respect. With her tunic filthy and torn, her dark hair in disarray and her bruises healing, his new slave looked like a wounded goddess. But she was just an ordinary woman. Why did she think she could defy him?

"Then let the games begin," he said, his voice thick with mockery.

"You think…this…this is a game?" she asked faintly.

The roughness of her voice reminded him of her body's weakened condition—a frailty her spirit clearly didn't share. Crouching beside her, he ran his forefinger over the yellowed bruise on her cheek. She closed her eyes and sighed as though his touch somehow soothed her.

Her guileless response unnerved him. The need to protect her enveloped him, a sensation he hadn't known since the deaths of his mother and sisters. As a slave, he'd been beaten on many occasions in an effort to conquer his will. That no one ever succeeded was a matter of pride for him. Much to his surprise, he had no wish to see this girl broken, either.

"Of course it's a game. And I will be the victor."

Defiance flamed in the depths of her large, doe-brown eyes. She didn't speak and he admired her restraint when he could see she wanted to flay him.

"You might as well give in now, my prize. I own you whether you will it or not."

He gripped her chin and forced her to look at him.

"Admit it," he said. "Then you can return to your sleep."

She shook her head. "No. No one owns me...no one but my God."

"And who might your god be? Jupiter? Apollo? Or maybe you worship the god of the sea. Do you think Neptune will rescue you?"

"The Christ."

Caros wondered if she were a fool or had a wish for death. "Say that to the wrong person, Pelonia, and you'll find yourself facing the lions."

"I already am."

He laughed. "So you think of me as a ferocious beast?"

Her silence amused him all the more. "Good. It suits me well to know you realize I'm untamed and capable of tearing you limb from limb."

"Then do your worst. Death is better...than being owned."

Caros suddenly noticed Pelonia had grown pale and weaker still.

He berated himself for depleting her meager strength when he should have been encouraging her to heal. He lifted her into his arms.

She weighed no more than a laurel leaf. Had he pushed her to the brink of death?

Holding her tight against his chest, he whispered near her ear. "Tell me, *mea carissima*. What can I do to aid you? What can I do to ease your plight?"

"Find...Tiberia," she whispered, the dregs of her strength draining away. "And free me."

* * * * *

Will Pelonia ever convince Caros of who she is and where she truly belongs? Or will their growing love bind her to him for all time?

Find out in
THE GLADIATOR
by Carla Capshaw
Available in November 2009
from Love Inspired® Historical

REQUEST YOUR FREE BOOKS!
2 FREE RIVETING INSPIRATIONAL NOVELS
PLUS 2 FREE MYSTERY GIFTS

YES! Please send me 2 FREE Love Inspired® Suspense novels and my 2 FREE mystery gifts (gifts are worth about $10). After receiving them, if I don't wish to receive any more books, I can return the shipping statement marked "cancel". If I don't cancel, I will receive 4 brand-new novels every month and be billed just $4.24 per book in the U.S. or $4.74 per book in Canada. That's a savings of over 20% off the cover price. It's quite a bargain! Shipping and handling is just 50¢ per book.* I understand that accepting the 2 free books and gifts places me under no obligation to buy anything. I can always return a shipment and cancel at any time. Even if I never buy another book, the two free books and gifts are mine to keep forever.

123 IDN EYM2 323 IDN EYNE

Name	(PLEASE PRINT)	
Address		Apt. #
City	State/Prov.	Zip/Postal Code

Signature (if under 18, a parent or guardian must sign)

Mail to Steeple Hill Reader Service:
IN U.S.A.: P.O. Box 1867, Buffalo, NY 14240-1867
IN CANADA: P.O. Box 609, Fort Erie, Ontario L2A 5X3

Not valid to current subscribers of Love Inspired Suspense books.

Want to try two free books from another series?
Call 1-800-873-8635 or visit www.morefreebooks.com

* Terms and prices subject to change without notice. Prices do not include applicable taxes. Sales tax applicable in N.Y. Canadian residents will be charged applicable provincial taxes and GST. Offer not valid in Quebec. This offer is limited to one order per household. All orders subject to approval. Credit or debit balances in a customer's account(s) may be offset by any other outstanding balance owed by or to the customer. Please allow 4 to 6 weeks for delivery. Offer available while quantities last.

Your Privacy: Steeple Hill Books is committed to protecting your privacy. Our Privacy Policy is available online at www.SteepleHill.com or upon request from the Reader Service. From time to time we make our lists of customers available to reputable third parties who may have a product or service of interest to you. If you would prefer we not share your name and address, please check here. ☐

LISUS09